P9-BZA-143

NAUGHTY MEN

Jan Springer
And
Lauren Agony

Erotic Futuristic Romance

New Concepts   Georgia

Be sure to check out our website for the very best in fiction at fantastic prices!

When you visit our webpage, you can:
* Read excerpts of currently available books
* View cover art of upcoming books and current releases
* Find out more about the talented artists who capture the magic of the writer's imagination on the covers
* Order books from our backlist
* Find out the latest NCP and author news--including any upcoming book signings by your favorite NCP author
* Read author bios and reviews of our books
* Get NCP submission guidelines
* And so much more!

We offer a 20% discount on all new Trade Paperback releases ordered from our website!

Be sure to visit our webpage to find the best deals in e-books and paperbacks! To find out about our new releases as soon as they are available, please be sure to sign up for our newsletter (http://www.newconceptspublishing.com/newsletter.htm) or join our reader group (http://groups.yahoo.com/group/new_concepts_pub/join)!

The newsletter is available by double opt in only and our customer information is *never* shared!

Visit our webpage at:
www.newconceptspublishing.com

Naughty Men is an original publication of NCP. This work has never before appeared in book form. This work is a novel. Any similarity to actual persons or events is purely coincidental.

New Concepts Publishing, Inc.
5202 Humphreys Rd.
Lake Park, GA 31636

ISBN 1-58608-740-1
March 2006 © Jan Springer & Lauren Agony
Cover art (c) copyright 2006 Kat Richards

All rights reserved, which includes the right to reproduce this book or portions thereof in any form whatsoever except as provided by the U.S. Copyright Law.

If you purchased this book without a cover you should be aware this book is stolen property.

NCP books are available at special quantity discounts for bulk purchases for sales promotions, premiums, fund raising, or educational use. For details, write, email, or phone New Concepts Publishing, Inc., 5202 Humphreys Rd., Lake Park, GA 31636; Ph. 229-257-0367, Fax 229-219-1097; orders@newconceptspublishing.com.

First NCP Trade Paperback Printing: March 2006

TABLE OF CONTENTS

LOVERBOY

Chapter One

Year 2043

Sex Squad Headquarters, Vermont, United States

"They call him Loverboy. He's six feet three inches tall and a hundred and eighty pounds of pure sex magnet. No woman can resist him." Lt. Jim McBride's husky voice curled through the briefing room, grabbing Detective Sky O'Kelley's attention.

The two male detectives sitting beside Sky nudged each other playfully and chuckled at Jim's description. Obviously they weren't taking this Loverboy fellow as seriously as they should be.

At their interruption, a dark look crept into Jim's gorgeous brown eyes. "You two giggly boys have something important to share with the rest of us?"

The two detectives frowned and shook their heads in embarrassment.

Jim nodded with satisfaction, then his intense gaze swooped onto Sky. His eyes softened a bit as he watched her, but the normal laugh lines at the corners of his mouth remained tight.

Bruised shadows hung beneath his eyes. Eyes that used to sparkle with desire for her. Now they held nothing but raw pain.

Hastily he looked away, leaving her with the impression she was being dismissed as if she were just another one of his "giggly boy" detectives, instead of the woman he had planned to marry ... up until a week ago.

Sky closed her eyes for a moment and tried to compose herself. Tears of regret burned at the back of her eyelids. She should have said yes to Jim's demands that she service him. It would have been so easy to put out that persistent ache between her legs. But she'd wanted to wait. Wait until she was one hundred percent sure about their relationship. Unfortunately, she'd said no one time too many and now she was alone.

"Here is a little history on Loverboy." Jim said. "Abandoned at birth, he was brought up in an orphanage by a passel of nuns. He was groomed to become a preacher. After several years of doing his duty to God, he left the church. For the past few years Loverboy has been living on a beach villa in California." Jim continued. "A couple of months ago a young woman went to the authorities claiming she was seduced by Loverboy and then kept at his beach villa against her will. She managed to escape but not before she discovered Loverboy was training men and women to become sex slaves.

As you all know, due to the overwhelming deaths from AIDS and other sexual diseases, not to mention the government's ravishing need for finding new forms of revenue, the government has legalized many things, including the registration of sex drugs, prostitution and sex slaves. However, avoiding payment of the income taxes obtained from such lucrative ventures is illegal. Loverboy has not filed any Sex Slave income tax returns. If what our source said is true and Loverboy is training slaves, he is in serious trouble for tax evasion.

The Chief wants two of our detectives to go in undercover. One will be a woman. A virgin. A virgin is required because rumor has it Loverboy knows one when he sees one. He can't resist them. And they can't resist him.

Apparently he is an exquisite lover. Once they have been with him they are hooked on sex. He then gives them intensive training in an eight week course in Pleasing.

He and one of his orphanage mates, Carmella, are the only instructors in his alleged training school."

The room was deathly quiet. Jim had captured everyone's attention.

"Our source discovered that the slave is guaranteed 100 percent employment at the end of his or her training period. Payment is $100,000 a year, with an option to continue the contract by either party at the end of that year."

"Get paid and get laid. Sounds like a hell of a good deal to me." One of the "giggly boys" whispered low enough so Jim couldn't hear.

"Beats the pay in the Sex Squad and you can screw your brains out." His companion eagerly whispered back.

Sky shook her head at the detective's insensitive comments.

Innocents were being sucked into a life of fast money without realizing the consequences. Didn't they want to wait to have sex until they fell in love? Or was she the only old fashioned girl left on this planet?

"A thorough inspection of Loverboy's villa showed nothing out of the ordinary going down. Unfortunately our source went missing shortly after she reported the incident to the authorities."

Sky couldn't help but feel regret at hearing the news about the woman. Loverboy must have heard about her going to the law and taken care of her in some horrid way.

"The woman is an only daughter of a high ranking government official. The father has hired us to track her down. Only the two people who accept the assignment will be given the identity of the woman."

"Do you believe she's still alive?" Sky asked quickly.

Jim seemed shocked by her question. The earlier warmth he'd shown in his eyes was replaced by ice. Sky shivered.

"She's alive. Most likely being trained as we speak."

"Are you saying she's being held against her will?"

"I mean she may have gone back on her own accord."

"No man is that powerful over a woman," Sky whispered with disbelief.

"Loverboy is," Jim stated firmly before focusing attention back onto the crowded room.

"Sex Squad officials believe Loverboy is now training slaves at another location. Surveillance has spotted him right here in Vermont. Living in a secluded farmhouse.

The other person we need is a male detective. He will go in undercover seeking employment as a slave. He must also keep an eye on the female detective while both search for the government official's daughter."

"What if the woman isn't there?" Sky asked.

"Then the undercover agents wait and ask questions without drawing attention to their true identity. They must be prepared to eagerly participate in the sex slave training. Without hesitation."

Sky felt her mouth drop open in shock. She barely heard the excited whispers shoot through the Briefing room as Jim ripped his gaze away from her and continued speaking.

"The female detective will target Loverboy and the male detective will target Carmella. Your assignment is two fold. Number One: Get yourself invited into his farmhouse and find out if he is in fact training sex slaves. And number two: Find the

woman and bring her out. If she's not there, find out where she is."
Jim's voice faded into the background as Sky examined
Loverboy's surveillance photo accompanying the notes they'd all
been given before the briefing had started.

She couldn't help but to inhale softly. She'd never seen such
sharp blue eyes. They reminded her of a fierce storm. Brooding.
Dark. Dangerous.

Short feathery blond hair framed a very masculine beach boy
face.

And those lush lips. So kissable.

A shiver of something she couldn't put her name to flickered up
her spine. It wasn't fear. This was a feeling she really liked.

Arousal?

Maybe.

Perhaps it was a need.

A need to meet this man and challenge his ability to make
innocent virgins into sex slaves.

She wanted to be the one to take Loverboy down… hopefully
not on top of her.

* * * *

"What the hell do you think you're doing taking on the
Loverboy assignment?" Jim yelled as he stormed into the
secluded conference room Sky was using to study the updated
Loverboy brief the Chief had given her.

Pure liquid heat streamed through her when she lifted her head
and stared head on into a pair of determined gritty eyes. He stood
so close she could smell his spicy cologne and feel the tension
radiating from his powerful body. A day's growth of stubble
covered his face, giving him a sexy aura.

Once again she found herself wishing she'd given into his
demands of making love to him.

An image of her cradled in his strong arms ... of Jim's powerful
hands kneading her tingling breasts, of him asking her if he could
make love to her right then and there.

His question had frightened her, and she'd told him to stop. He
had. And then he'd left. Right after telling her he couldn't wait for
her any longer.

"You're not taking this assignment. Is that clear?" he snapped,
and Sky blinked away the vision. Anger at his command welled.

"Don't tell me what to do Jim McBride! You lost that right
when you canceled our engagement."

"Oh? And now you'd rather get fucked by Loverboy instead of making love to me?"

"Maybe he'll show me a few tricks." She breathed.

His eyes darkened into dangerous slits. She loved it when he was mad. It gave him so much power over her. A power to do anything he wanted... but he'd never had the balls to do it.

With a quick move that took Sky by surprise, Jim grabbed her around the waist and yanked her clear out of her seat.

He captured her startled cry in his mouth as his warm lips crushed over hers.

She could taste his fierce need as his hot, thick tongue slipped into her mouth. Strong and demanding, he probed, pushed, circled and finally mated with her tongue.

Her blood roared in her ears. Her breasts jumped to attention.

Her nipples tightened. Tingled. Sparkled with desire as they flattened against his hard chest.

She'd been in his arms before. Many times. She'd enjoyed his tender kisses. Wished he'd be more aggressive.

Today, it looked as if she just might get her wish. Today, she might have pushed him a little too far.

There was a sharp edge to this kiss.

A tinge of desperation. A hint of domination.

She liked this new Jim. She liked him a lot.

Her body melted against his hot length. She reached up, feathered her fingers through his raven black hair and cupped the back of his warm head, drawing him closer.

His powerful masculine scent drugged her like a fine wine and his body heat zipped through her thin blouse, setting her flesh on fire.

His mouth tasted dark, dangerous and oh so delicious. So yummy she wanted to devour him.

All of him.

She ached to taste his chest, suckle his pebble-hard nipples, swallow his sweet cum as his powerful penis thrust in and out of her hungry mouth.

The shocking thoughts made Sky shiver with a frenzied excitement. She felt her self control slipping.

She should make him stop. Make him stop just like all the other times.

This time she couldn't.

She wanted more from him. So much more.

Her nerves were short circuiting. Everywhere.

Every inch of her tingled. She ached to be touched. To be tasted. To be fucked.

What was happening to her? Who cared? As long as he kept doing it.

A noise rumbled deep in her throat. It was a sensual sound she'd never heard before.

Jim must have heard it too because his kiss intensified. His lips became more demanding. Dominating. Intoxicating.

She tried to match his strength, but she couldn't. He overpowered her senses. She was lost. Mindless with aching sensations she'd never felt before.

His right hand left her waist and trailed a searing line up her bare hot skin to slip under her blouse. In a flash, his fingers dove below the lace material of her bra and headed straight for her left nipple.

He found it.

The instant he touched her very tip, a jolt of blazing pleasure sliced through her breast and another bolt exploded like lightning between her legs.

She arched her back against his hand, increasing the exquisite pressure as his heated fingers became trapped against her bare breast and his chest.

Somehow he maneuvered his finger and thumb around her hardened nub and he squeezed. A punishing pinch. Firm enough to cause a spectacular tenderness to replace the arousal.

Immediately his cruel touch melted into a semi rough caress as he began to rub and roll her now aching nipple between his thumb and finger.

She bolted at the unfamiliar sensations pulsing through her body. The way her breast swelled beneath his brutal touch made her squirm. His other hand slid tighter around her waist, pulling her closer to his heated body.

His steady pressure on her nipple finally produced that familiar feverish yearning between her legs.

She sucked in a breath when his hand left her aching breast and attacked her other nipple. In moments, both nipples screamed in agony.

He left her breasts quivering and aching with need as his hot hands blazed along her bare belly, making her shiver in anticipation. Long fingers hooked her waistband. Cool air slapped against her legs as he pulled down her pants and underwear.

His hot hands cupped her bare ass and she was being lifted upward. He plopped her crudely onto the coldness of the table and uncapped his hands. With one professional sweep, he ripped her pants and underwear off her legs.

With one knee, he forced her legs apart and moved between them, pressing his shockingly massive erection against her exposed and aching pussy.

The size of his bulge frightened her. And it exhilarated her!

She inhaled sharply at the burning wave of lust rippling through her cunt like a sparkler on the Fourth of July. Wetness trickled between her legs. It wasn't enough to extinguish the growing ball of fire.

His kiss deepened, tilting her world.

A hot callused finger skimmed along the inside of her thigh, leaving a trail of excitement in it's wake. She shuddered at his delicious touch. It felt so good.

He ripped his mouth away from hers and whispered hoarsely into her ear. "Don't you realize what you've just volunteered for?"

His hot finger parted the swollen folds of her labia. A searing electrical current of passion shot through her cunt as he began to rub her ultra sensitive nub above her clit.

She let go of him, threw back her head and cried out from the intensity of his violent touch. She didn't care who heard. She was beyond caring. She'd entered a new world. A dangerous world of pleasure.

"Loverboy will take one peek at your sweet innocent girl next door looks and fuck you."

Jim's pressure on her nub increased. His touch became electric. Savage.

Sky couldn't help but cry out again as violent sensations pulsed inside her womb.

"Is this what you want him to do to you, Sky?"

"Yes!" she hissed.

Her legs trembled as another wave of ecstasy assaulted her. Her hips surged upward against his hot finger. Begging for more.

She bucked on the table as a finger plunged inside her wet cunt. White hot splendor crashed around her. Another burning finger plunged inside. And then another. And another.

He filled her aggressively. His masculine strength hammering in and out.

Faster.

Faster.

Until peak after shocking peak swept over her. They kept coming. Crashing into her. Around her. Waves of exploding heat.

They frightened her.

Jim kept pumping. Her hips kept grinding. She couldn't stop herself!

Something was coming! Something beautiful. And scary. Fierce. Unbearable pleasure took control.

Sky tightened her eyes. Her heart crashed against her chest.

Jim quickened his pace. Within seconds, a deep wrenching explosion ripped through her cunt.

Sky screamed.

She began to shake violently.

"Go with it, Sky. Let yourself go with it," Jim's soft voice urged.

"I can't!" She gasped. Frantic for air.

She reached out to Jim. Clutched his strong shoulders. Dug her fingernails deep into his thick muscles.

"Ride with it! Trust me."

"Oh God! Help me!"

It was insane. Unbearable. Pain. Ecstasy. Both.

"Let yourself go," he whispered.

Sky followed his voice and did what she was told. She let go.

A fierce wave swallowed her. Bright stars burst around her. She tumbled with such unimaginable joy, she couldn't help but sob at its brutality.

She didn't know how long the ecstasy ripped her apart, but finally it was over and she began to float.

She could hear Jim's heavy breathing. Could hear herself panting.

Hot tears dripped down her cheeks. Her cunt muscles shivered and shuddered around Jim's fingers.

She felt dazed. Wiped out. Satisfied.

Wonderful.

God! That was fantastic!

She held onto Jim's massive shoulders until the hot flush claiming her body began to subside.

Then she loosened her grip.

"I won't ask if it was good. I can see it on your face. You look like a woman who has been properly finger fucked."

His voice was tender, sweet despite his words.

Reality set in. Oh God! What had she done?

She was sitting on a desk in a room in the middle of Sex Squad Headquarters with a man's fingers sticking in her cunt.

What if someone walked in on them?

Having sex on the job was illegal. They'd be fired.

Despite her uneasiness, she wanted Jim's warm fingers to stay inside her. He felt so nice. So filling. So natural.

"Sky, look at me."

She opened her eyes and her breath caught at the darkness of desire brewing in those brown depths.

"Loverboy or some other man will fuck you until you're as mindless as you just were. Do you see how easy it is for a man to take down a sexually inexperienced woman like you? Do you?" Concern marred Jim's rugged face.

Maybe he was right. Maybe this assignment was too dangerous. Look what had just happened to her. She'd loved what Jim had done to her. She wanted him to do it again. And again.

Doubt mushroomed. She almost caved in. Almost.

"Thanks for the vote of confidence," she said tightly as she fought back tears of betrayal. She thought he'd wanted to please her, not teach her a lesson.

"Dammit, Sky. Don't do this."

"It's done."

He cursed beneath his breath. A sucking sound shot through the air as he slid his fingers out of her drenched cunt.

She wished he could stay inside her. She wanted more of this ecstasy. Much more.

"I guess I was wrong about you, Sky. I'm glad I finally came to my senses and left you. Good luck. You're going to need it!"

He turned and stomped toward the unlocked door.

Son of a bitch! People might see her like this!

Sky jumped off the table, her shaky legs almost crumbling as her feet landed on the floor.

Quickly, she picked up her clothing and covered herself. Suddenly she realized she wanted to give in to Jim. Wanted him to fuck her. Wanted him to take her virginity. To take her back into the dangerous world of pleasure.

Now! "Jim! Please, don't go!"

The door slammed shut behind his broad back.

Too late.

The tiny sliver of hope she'd been harboring about them getting back together walked out the door with him.

Wiping away the hot tears streaming down her face, she donned her damp underwear and stepped into her pants.

Looking at the door, Sky squared her shoulders in defiance.

Jim McBride had just given her a lesson she wouldn't easily forget. She'd be on her guard from here on out.

Chapter Two

Jim McBride hunched against the cold brick wall of the deserted men's bathroom.

His heart crashed against his chest, his breath escaping in shallow gasps.

Damn! What the hell did he think he was doing trying to change Sky's mind? He should know by now she was one stubborn woman. Once she made up her mind about something there was no stopping her.

He really shouldn't be worried about her. As inexperienced as she was sexually, she was a damned good detective. She'd always been able to take care of herself.

So, why was he worried now?

Uneasiness pricked through him. Anything could go wrong, that's why. She was a virgin for god's sake. Sexually inexperienced. He would lose her if Loverboy got his hands on her.

Jim had read the Loverboy file. Loverboy targeted virgins. Wooed them. Seduced them. Fucked them until they were hooked to his intense lovemaking and then they did whatever he asked. Obviously he was great in bed if he could get women to willingly become sex slaves.

No way in hell was Jim going to let the woman he loved go down that road.

In desperation he'd stormed into the Squad room Sky had been using. He'd found her ogling Loverboy's photo, her cheeks rosy red, big blue eyes wide with want.

She'd looked so desirable. He'd wanted her so bad, his cock ached. He'd wanted her naked. Right there on the desk. Squirming and moaning as he forced his cock into her. His long fierce strokes plunging into her pussy, making her scream with pleasure.

He'd wanted to worship her. To brand her as his own. To remove that look of interest brewing in her eyes over Loverboy's photo.

The burning anger and her comment about Loverboy teaching her how to make love had overruled his usual control to the point where he'd grabbed her and kissed her.

Her sweet scent had drowned him. Made him heady with need. He'd managed to thwart his own desires in order to pleasure her. He'd done it by attacking her passion bud. She'd melted under his onslaught.

Surprised she'd let him touch her down there, his fingers had grown bold and he'd slipped past her swollen nether lips and into her hot channel. She'd been tight, but wetter than sin and had accepted his other fingers with relative ease. He'd begun ramming her. Again and again.

He'd felt the exact instant she'd lost control and given into the pleasure he was offering. She'd spread her legs wider, grabbed a hold of him. Dug her nails into his shoulders.

Heck! He could still feel the pain of where her fingernails had dug into his skin.

Ravishing agony had scrunched up her pretty face. Her sexy moans of disbelief had urged him on. He'd pumped harder. Faster.

Finally she'd screamed and climaxed. Her cunt muscles contracting and spasming around his fingers.

He'd wanted her to get an idea of what she was missing. Of what she'd been denying him. He'd done the job. Quite well.

He'd changed her attitude toward sex. Seen the magical sparkle of satisfaction in those big blue aroused eyes. The lovely blush of embarrassment on her face when she realized she'd lost control and given him her trust.

Jim closed his eyes at the sweet memory and leaned his head against the cold brick wall behind him.

Dammit!

He could still taste her sweetness on his lips. Feel the warmth of her cunt burning into his palm. The wetness of her cunt juices on his fingers.

He'd wanted more than anything to remove his fingers and slip his aching shaft into her succulent cunt. He'd been close to doing it.

So damn close. But it would have been a mistake.

From the start of their relationship she'd made it perfectly clear she wouldn't give herself to a man until she was sure she loved him. Finally a few weeks ago she'd said she loved him. He'd been so happy he'd proposed right away. Hadn't given it a second thought. He knew he loved her and he wanted to make love to her as soon as possible. Last week they'd gone to a wedding of a mutual friend. They'd watched the bride and groom sexually consummate their wedding in front of the eager preacher, friends and family as was required by law. The sensuous cries of the bride and the erotic groans of the groom had rung through the church making Jim so hot when he'd gotten Sky alone in her apartment that night he'd tried to seduce her. It had almost worked until she'd suddenly told him she wanted to wait to have sex with him until their wedding.

Cripes! He'd waited so long to be with her and then suddenly she told him she needed an extension. Damned it was frustrating.

He craved to make her his wife. Wanted to see her face flushed with desire and to hear those sexy little moans deep in her throat every morning as he made love to her. He wanted to father her children. If he had his way they'd have lots of kids.

There was no way he'd let Loverboy stop him from his dreams.

Jim swallowed as an idea hit him. Suddenly he knew exactly what he needed to do.

* * * *

One week later...

Awareness coursed through Sky the instant she saw Loverboy enter the smoky bar room. He reminded her of a sleek panther hunting for a mate as he strode confidentially to the polished mahogany bar. The bartender grinned a friendly welcome and slapped down a foamy beer in front of Loverboy.

Sky didn't miss the appetizing way his tight jeans hugged his cute buns as he sat on the barstool or the way those extra large shoes kissed the floor.

You know what they say about a man's feet. Big feet. Big cock.

A spark of excitement shot through her body. Her gaze moved up toward his beer mug. To those fingers clasped around the frosty mug.

Long, thick fingers. Just like Jim's.

She wondered if Loverboy's fingers would elicit the same exciting sensations as Jim's had. Somehow she didn't think so. Jim McBride was the man for her. She knew it now. Unfortunately it was too late. Jim had cut her out of his life.

Sky swallowed and pressed her cool glass of tequila against her suddenly hot forehead.

Damn that Jim McBride!

Ever since his lethal fingers had fucked her, she hadn't been able to think of anything else but sex.

Sex. Sex. Sex.

It was as if he'd unleashed her carnal side. Ripped away her confidence and made her addicted to...well, sex.

A friend of hers had once told her, "The minute you get properly fucked by a man, you're hooked. Addicted to the high of sex."

Ain't that the truth.

Over the past week she'd fantasized about Jim. All the time. She'd even dreamed of how it would be to make love to him.

Plunging his hard dick into her hot cunt or her eager mouth. Or maybe her ass?

She closed her eyes and tried to keep the dark fantasies from crowding into her brain. She needed to concentrate on her job. Not the lust screaming through her system.

Sky rolled her cool glass over her hot cheek, opened her eyes and watched Loverboy.

Tonight, he seemed different from his photo and from the other nights she'd followed him.

Tonight, he looked bigger. Taller. More powerful. Damn sexy.

Muscles bulged in his strong arms as he hoisted his mug to his lips.

Full lips. Kissable lips.

Down girl.

The next time she saw Jim she'd give him a piece of her mind for introducing her to sex. Up until his impromptu performance she'd been quite content masturbating on her own. Thank you very much.

Thinking of Jim conjured up the way she'd been so nervous when she'd shown up at Sex Squad Headquarters tonight to tell the Chief she was making her move in less than two hours. She'd wanted to know who the male backup would be. He'd reassured her a man would be in place by the time she got to the farmhouse.

She could have phoned and told him she was making her move tonight, but she'd hoped to see Jim. To see what he could have had if he'd just waited until their wedding.

She'd wanted to flaunt herself in his face. She'd had her hair cut and styled and colored. She'd gone from mousy brown to sexy blonde.

She hadn't seen Jim but the Chief had commented about her new appearance and the way his gaze had raked over every inch of her body, she knew he liked what he saw.

She'd picked a tight black leather skirt that showed off her wide hips. A matching pair of pumps, a plain white very see through blouse, and a black string bow tie. She'd opted for no bra and no underwear. Those were the two things she was self conscious about. The thought of possibly showing Loverboy her cunt in order to get him interested, and the fact that her blouse left little to anyone's imagination.

Hopefully it would grab Loverboy's attention.

By the way the male customer's eyes had stalked her tonight when she'd entered the bar she knew she'd done something right.

During her research phase, she'd followed Loverboy and quickly discovered he was a creature of routine.

Every night he visited the same ten bars. He acted like a regular customer, ordered a beer. Chatted pleasantly with a bartender.

Ten minutes later, he'd leave. Without drinking his beer.

She'd checked the financial situations of all ten bars and a pattern had emerged.

All the bars were owned by the prospective bartenders. All businesses were in financial trouble.

The way Sky figured it, Loverboy targeted these bars because of their financial distress. The barkeeps kept their eyes open for potential victims and Loverboy paid them generously.

Tonight, she'd picked bar number seven in the string. The smallest business with the largest debt. She'd already given the bartender her sob story over a couple of potent tequilas.

Now she waited anxiously for the barkeep to hopefully mention her to Loverboy.

It didn't take long.

Unexpectedly Loverboy turned his head and they made eye contact. His look was intense. Intoxicating. Her pulse skittered. She forgot to breathe.

His ravishing gaze slid from her face to skim along the length of her neck, over her chest. She swore she could feel his eyes softly caress her breasts.

Her nipples peaked. Hardened. They ached to be touched.

God!

Jim had been right. There was something about this man.

She needed to be very careful. Needed to get a grip.

Loverboy was forbidden territory.

And he was heading straight for her!

"You're a beautiful woman obviously in need of a man." he whispered into her ear as he sat down on the barstool beside her.

His breath smelled delicately of beer. Mixed with his own unique scent, it went straight to her head like a shot of whiskey. A tinge of dizziness swept through her and she held tight to the edge of the bar.

Easy girl. You're here for a reason.

Sky swallowed. Hard.

She lifted her head and looked up at him under her lashes and smiled seductively.

"What makes you think I'm in need of a man?"

"The way your nipples are practically popping out of your blouse. Aching to be caressed. Suckled. Worshipped."

Mercy! He had a way with words.

He continued, his breath a whisper against her face, "Your eyes are shining brightly with a hunger for sex. I'm sure if I touched your clit, you'd be wet for me."

"And if I reached over…" Sky swallowed back her fear and forced herself to keep her eyes on his sexy mouth as she boldly cupped her hand over the giant hot bulge pressing against his pants.

The man was huge! Almost as big as Jim. She couldn't resist squeezing his hard jewels.

Loverboy's lips twitched slightly.

Amazing.

A tough man like himself aroused by her touch.

Feminine power surged in Sky giving her back some of that confidence she'd lost to Jim when he'd finger fucked her last week.

Sky's smile grew.

"Your place or mine?" she asked as she released her grip from the intoxicating bulge.

Loverboy returned her smile, and Sky inhaled sharply. He looked absolutely cuddly when he smiled like that, but she noticed his smile didn't reach his cool blue eyes.

"I'm sorry, I don't do virgins."

Sky blinked in surprise. That's not what she'd heard. She could feel the Loverboy case begin to slip through her fingers.

"I'm sorry," he said. "I've offended you."

"No. No. I'm the one who's sorry. I came on too strong. I've never done this sort of thing before. Temporary insanity. A momentary lapse of judgment." She fingered her now warm tequila glass wondering what she should do next.

"That's quite understandable. You want to get back at your ex-fiancé. Show him you've decided you'd rather get fucked by someone else because he couldn't wait for you."

"That's very perceptive."

"Actually, the bartender mentioned you had some trouble with your boyfriend. It's very admirable you wanted to remain a virgin until your wedding nuptials. He should have been very proud to wait for you. To be given the privilege to go where no man has gone before."

Despite trying to appear sophisticated, she couldn't help the hot flush from flooding her face. When she'd sobbed her story to the bartender, she hadn't been the least bit embarrassed. What she'd told him was part of her strategy in getting noticed by Loverboy. She'd stuck to the truth as much as possible, lessening her chances of saying the wrong thing and tipping off Loverboy she was a Sex Squad cop.

"Ah. A virgin blush. The most beautiful thing for a man to see."

"I intend on rectifying that problem soon," Sky stated.

"So the bartender told me."

"And since you don't do virgins..." Sky looked around the smoky room. "I'm sure there will be another candidate along soon enough.

"I think maybe I can help you... in some other way."

She narrowed her eyes trying to appear curious.

"How?"

"The bartender mentioned you got laid off last week. I may be able to find you employment."

"Are you serious?"

"I plan on running a school in the area."

Sky ran a finger along the edge of her glass, trying hard not to show her excitement.

"What kind of school?"

"How to please men and women."

"Excuse me?"

"I plan on training sex slaves. I'm looking around for some recruits. Are you interested?"

Her heart picked up speed. "I've heard they make great pay."

"They do."

"I might be interested."

"What's your name, hon?"

"Sky. Sky Blue." It was the cover name the department had come up with for her.

"How about you come to my farm and meet the class? You can participate in some lessons and if you don't like them, we go our separate ways".

"How do I know you're not just going to take me out somewhere, fuck me, kill me and get rid of my body?"

Loverboy grinned and shook his head slowly. "Now that would be bad for my business. Everyone here sees me talking to you. If you leave with me, they'll see that, too. If you suddenly go missing, there are a lot of witnesses that saw us together. The last thing I need is to have the cops asking a lot of questions and scaring off potential clients, right?"

Sky nodded her head. "I suppose."

"So, want to try the school out?"

"On one condition."

"Anything."

"You buy me one more Tequila for the road." Heaven knew she was going to need it.

Chapter Three

Although Sky felt flushed, she didn't think it had too much to do with the alcohol and more to do with this virile man sitting on the truck bench seat beside her.

Something about him made her heart gallop at full speed with both excitement and fear.

Her ploy had worked. She'd been invited to Loverboy's farmhouse. But what if he decided he did "do" virgins and wanted her?

Although she knew self defense, she didn't know if she could fend this big guy off her if he decided he did want her.

"Where you from, Sky?"

"New Hampshire," she lied.

"That's not far from here. Just across the state line. What kind of work do you do?"

A perfectly normal question. So why were beads of perspiration popping out on her brow?

"I tend to be a gypsy. Drift here and there. Work at whatever I can find. Waitressing mostly."

"Any family?"

"Mom was it. She died a few years ago. Way too old for her age. Worked herself to death juggling three jobs so she could bring me up with the things she never had."

"Your father?"

Sky forced herself to keep her emotion in check at that question.

"Never knew him. Took off when mom found out she was pregnant. Joined the army and she never heard from him again."

"I see."

Sky inhaled a quiet sob. What she'd told him was the truth, except for the gypsy and waitressing parts. That had been her mom. Dragging her all over the States, working here and there. Doing a little prostituting when funds were low. She even read tarot cards to raise money.

"I suppose that's why you've hung on to your virginity so long. Can't trust a man."

"Can't trust condoms or The Pill or The One Year Injection. They aren't one hundred percent reliable."

"Well, there always is that chance that one of those little buggers will wiggle through and you'll end up like your mom, right?"

Sky nodded. Hit the nail on the head with that one.

"Yet you want to lose your virginity to a stranger?"

Although she felt quite jittery and a bit embarrassed at his prying questions, Sky tilted her chin upward in a brave show of defiance. Oh, the things a Sex Squad Cop had to do to take down her man.

"That's right. I aim to get fucked. Good and hard."

Oh God! She couldn't believe she'd just said that. She must be hornier than she thought.

"You're not afraid to get pregnant anymore?"

No, because I'll be gone before the pleasantries begin... hopefully.

Sky shrugged. "If it happens, it happens. It's time to get on with life. I want to experience being a woman."

"Why not ask your ex-fiancé to do the honors? I mean he's been waiting for so long. I'm sure he'd be more that willing."

"He's long gone. Out of the picture. He obviously couldn't wait." She suddenly wished Jim was tailing them right now. Keeping an eye on her. She couldn't help but to glance at the side view mirror. No lights beckoned to her.

"I'm sure we can find the right man to do the job, for you. We want your first time to be... memorable."

He glanced over at her and winked.

Sky's breath caught at the gesture.

What did he mean by that remark? Had he changed his mind? Was he insinuating he was going to do the job?

Oh God!

What if he offered? What if she accepted? Sky shook her head.

No! She couldn't accept an offer from Loverboy, that is, if he made one.

She needed to stick to her principles. But what was wrong with her even toying with the idea?

She knew why. Ever since Jim's finger fucking had introduced her to the world of sex she wanted more. More of the wild pleasure. More of losing control and trusting a man. She wanted Jim.

Yes, she was definitely addicted.

Sky's gaze drew to Loverboy's long fingers curled around the steering wheel. Wetness pooled in her underwear at the thought of Loverboy touching her down there.

Her cunt felt hot and she could even feel her vaginal muscles contracting at the mere thought of Loverboy finger fucking her.

Oh boy, was she ever lusting after this guy. Maybe it was the tequila she'd been drinking tonight. Research proved drinking alcohol affected the part of the brain that increases sexual awareness.

That's what it was, the tequila. Then again, maybe not.

Maybe it was Loverboy's unique body chemistry. Jim had mentioned something along those lines during briefing. She couldn't deny something oozed from Loverboy. He did smell delicious, but not as yummy as Jim.

To her surprise, Loverboy's arm lifted and curled around her shoulders drawing her against him. She felt the urge to pull away but didn't. If she did, she would only tip him off.

Best to stay right here and pretend she was truly interested in him.

Up ahead in the darkness, Loverboy's secluded farmhouse appeared. The porch light shone across the yard, giving Sky a good glimpse of the building. White paint curled off in long strips, revealing an ugly dark gray beneath the sidings. Some shutters were missing, others crooked. What once must have been a garden lining the front porch was now overgrown with weeds. Although the house appeared neglected, Sky saw the potential.

A few slaps of white paint on the walls, rosy pink on the shutters and pretty wildflowers in the garden and the place would look friendly not brooding.

A buttery glow splashed from most of the windows. As Loverboy drove the pickup truck into the yard, Sky spied a shadowy figure, watching from a second floor window. A man by the looks of it, but he quickly vanished.

Two women lounged on a couple of porch wicker chairs. When they spotted the truck, they raced down the stairs toward them.

They were young. Very young and very pretty.

A niggle of low self esteem slipped over Sky. These two women were gorgeous compared to her. They were thin with seductive curves and well toned.

Model material.

With those gorgeous creatures around him no wonder Loverboy had refused to fuck her.

The smile of appreciation on Loverboy's face proved Sky's point. She was surprised when a hint of jealousy skittered through her the instant the two women latched onto him as he stepped out of the truck.

How cozy. Just like clinging vines.

Her cop brain shifted into gear. Who were these two young women? They were barely out of their teens and willing to become sex slaves.

Why were they so happy to see Loverboy? And why couldn't they seem to keep their hands off his powerful body?

"We're glad you're back," a very pretty auburn haired woman with a heart shaped face said.

"Hi Carmella. Hi Loren. You gals been practicing your lessons while I was away?"

"We have," the auburn haired said. "Loren was showing the new guy some of what she's learned so far with her tongue." Sky didn't miss the sparkles in both their eyes or the reddish glow to their cheeks as they spoke of the newcomer.

He had to be her backup from Sex Squad Headquarters.

"Did you bring the presents?" Carmella asked.

"In the back of the trunk."

The two women squealed and giggled as Loverboy led them to the back and lifted a large paper bag.

From it he withdrew two long white boxes.

Long stemmed roses? Maybe. But she wouldn't bet on it.

Sky climbed out of the truck and joined the happy trio.

Carmella finally acknowledged Sky by giving her a quick once over.

"I see you've found our last student." She said, returning her attention to Loverboy.

"Ladies, this is Sky. She's going to try out some lessons and see if she's interested."

"You're not sure you want to be a sex slave?" Carmella asked.

"She's pretty sure. It's just she's a virgin." Loverboy said quickly.

Sky didn't miss the strange look Carmella threw at him.

"I see," she said coldly.

"Lessons start in an hour. Spread the word," Loverboy stated firmly.

Carmella stared at him for a long moment. Sky could see anger in her eyes, but she said nothing. Obviously there was some discord between the two partners.

The two women brushed past Sky, and she couldn't help but notice the diagrams on one of the white boxes. Her mouth dropped open in shock.

Oh my God!

Loverboy had just given them vibrators.

When the two women slipped inside the farmhouse, Loverboy shifted the paper bag in his arms and grinned at her.

"I've already got a mistress lined up for Loren. She had one look at Loren's photo and fell in love with her. How about you? Do you by any chance prefer women over men?"

Shit! What was the right answer?

"Depends who pays more," she answered carefully.

"That's what I like to hear. A woman who is open minded. You'll go far in this business if you don't limit your possibilities."

Sky forced herself to return his smile.

He waved his hand in a sweeping gesture toward the farmhouse. "After you," he said.

Sky swallowed as she passed him and the full paper bag he held in his hands.

God! Vibrators!

She wondered what type they were. Were they the same kind she used? A delicious seven inch long dong, one inch wide with the utmost in satisfying power.

Unbidden came a vision of Jim lying naked on a bed. Tangled sheets wrapped around his muscular thighs. A tempting glimpse of dark curly hair, a sizable penis. Hooded dark eyes searing into hers as he plunged the vibrator deep into her cunt.

"Looks like the crew has already turned in to prepare."

"Prepare?" Sky asked as they entered the deserted farmhouse.

"For their lessons."

Right. Should she ask him questions about these lessons? Or would she appear too curious?

Loverboy's voice broke into her thoughts. "Don't worry, Sky. I'll introduce you to the lessons slowly. See if you like it. Then I'll give you more details about the job."

Oh dear. How in the world was she going to be able to go through with this? Or maybe the question would be, how far was she willing to go?

"Ah, here is the new recruit," Loverboy cooed as he looked up the steep staircase.

Sky followed his gaze and her mouth went dry with shock as she caught sight of a man standing in the shadows. Although she couldn't see his face, she recognized his well built physique. Remembered those slim hips, the lean torso, wide shoulders, those lethal long fingers.

Oh-my-God!

Jim!

"Would you like something to eat? Or drink?" Loverboy broke into her thoughts.

Her heart pounded insanely against her chest, and she realized she'd been holding her breath.

"No thanks, I'm rather tired. If you wouldn't mind, I'd like to lie down awhile. I must have drank too many tequilas."

The sooner she ditched Loverboy, the sooner Jim and she could take a look around and hopefully find something about the missing woman.

"Jim!" Loverboy called up the stairs. "Would you mind showing Sky to her room? It's the last one on the end of the hall. Right side."

"Sure. Come on up, Sky."

Sky shivered at the sound of Jim's husky voice curling out of the shadows.

His hot stare cascaded over her in violent waves as she ascended the stairs. The walls of the staircase seemed to swoop in around her, and her body picked up a lovely hum the closer she got to him.

When she reached the top of the stairs, he stood right there in front of her, barring her way with his muscular body.

The intense way he gazed at her made her remember the new blonde look she'd taken and the revealing clothes she wore. She'd never seen him looking at her like this before. It was a possessive stare. A wildly erotic glare she rather liked.

Hints of his intoxicating male scent swarmed over her, making a deep intimate part of her spark to life. Making her want to curl her arms around his neck and kiss away the leashed anger evaporating from his magnificent body.

Medium length brown hair was brushed back off his face giving him a bad boy Mafia appearance. He wore a black short sleeved t-shirt which showed off his powerful arms. And his jeans were so tight, she immediately noticed the large bulge between his legs.

"You like what you see?" His voice was dangerously calm and it made her gaze snap back to his face. Back to those gorgeous brown eyes that oozed naked desire.

"Why didn't you tell me you were the backup?" she whispered.

"Didn't have the time," he said thickly as his hungry gaze traveled over her see-through blouse. Then he spoke louder. "You're room is this way, ma'am."

She followed him down the long hallway, watching his buns shift against those tight jeans as he walked. Her cunt quivered with anticipation when she envisioned herself cupping his bare ass as he pressed his hot penis into her.

Oh shit!

She'd better control herself and keep her mind on her job. Or better yet find one of those vibrators Loverboy was so eagerly passing around and feed her sexual appetite.

Jim stopped at the end of the hall, opened the door and flicked on a light.

Sky couldn't help but to inhale at the beauty of the cozy room. Virgin white cutwork linens adorned large windows. Huge pillows edged in scalloped lace lay on the white bed comforter. The bed itself was made of knotty pine with an unusual headboard shaped like a wagon wheel.

Sky walked over to it and ran her fingers over the intricate design on the sturdy spindles.

"It's beautiful. So rustic and romantic."

"A room fit for a princess. And every beautiful princess should have one of these," Jim said. From behind his back he produced one of those long stemmed white boxes.

Sky's heart picked up speed as he held it out to her. For the longest time she could only stare at it. Then she accepted the package, trying hard to act sophisticated. But the burning in her face gave her away.

He grinned and his sexy smile made her heart do a little double flip.

"It's compliments of the house. Last one."

"Not anymore."

She ignored his puzzled expression and dropped the vibrator onto the night table.

When she looked up, he pressed his fingers to his lips in warning. Immediately she knew something was up.

"Thanks for showing me to my room. Um, perhaps we can see each other during the lessons tonight?" she teased.

"Looking forward to it ma'am."

He strolled across the floor, opened the door, peeked out to see if anyone was there and then closed the door with enough noise to indicate he'd left. Then he led her into the bathroom.

Closing the door quietly, he turned on the water taps. Dumping her purse on the bathroom counter, she joined Jim as he scanned the bathroom for listening devices or other monitoring systems. When they found nothing, he switched on the bathroom fan as a precaution and turned to her.

His clean, male scent wrapped around her, making her want to touch him. Making her heart race wildly. Making the room suddenly feel too damn small.

The sexual tension between them flared to life.

"I did a search of a couple of the bedrooms and found some listening devices," he said. "Obviously, Loverboy and Carmella don't trust too easily."

"In their line of alleged illegal activities, I wouldn't either. How long have you been here?"

"Long enough to have not seen Sally Green."

Sky shook her head. "I still can't believe she's the missing woman."

"Daughter of our own boss, who the hell knew? No wonder he wanted to keep her identity under wraps."

"She is a beautiful young woman. I'm not surprised Loverboy targeted her," Sky said.

Jim moved closer to her, his warm chest mere inches from her breasts.

"You did a good job getting Loverboy's attention yourself, Sky, but can you handle what's coming next?"

"What's the matter? You can't deal with a little bit of sex?" she purred.

He bristled visibly at her remark. "Looks like you're already into this sex game, Sky. The way you were practically sitting in Loverboy's lap when you two drove up in the truck, I could see the sparks shooting out the windows. If there was a gas leak around here, we would have all been blown to kingdom come."

"We were just getting acquainted. Like you were doing with that Loren woman's tongue."

He arched a dark eyebrow at her. "You heard about that did you? Any objections?"

"Why should I care? You're a free agent again. Just like I am."

The sizzling tension between them thickened. His voice lowered to little more than a husky whisper. "You still want to go through with this assignment? Even if it means you might lose your virginity before you leave this farmhouse."

"Is that a promise?" she found herself saying.

His eyes darkened and its intensity startled her. "Is that an invitation?"

"What do you think?"

"Don't toy with me, Sky. You may not like the results."

"You don't scare me, big guy," Sky breathed.

A dangerous shiver of excitement rippled through her body when she read the intent in his eyes. The son of a bitch was going to kiss her.

Before she could protest, not that she wanted to, his hands roughly cupped her face and he lowered his head toward hers. His warm mouth sealed over hers in a hard possessive way.

A little too hard. A little too firm. A little too perfect.

No more mister nice guy. He was a man who knew what he wanted. And the way he was kissing her, he wanted her.

Her arms slipped around his neck. Her fingers feathering his soft hair as she cupped the back of his head.

His kiss intensified, making her feel punch drunk. Need for him made her breath catch. Made her pulse quicken.

She parted her lips, allowing him access to her mouth. When he came in, the provocative heat of his tongue slammed against hers. She moaned shamelessly at the deep pleasure of it.

Trembling male hands unbuttoned her blouse, all the while he kept his hot mouth expertly moving over hers. She savored the sexy flavor of his soft full lips. Loved the coiled need unwrapping inside her cunt. Felt the quivers of desire shivering through Jim's kiss.

Cool air slammed against her bare breasts, making her nipples stab against the coarse material of his shirt as he tugged her blouse over her shoulders, allowing it to slip off.

She arched against him as his hot hands cupped her breasts, his thumbs gently caressing her stiff nipples until they were aching with need. The intimate gesture soon set her cunt on fire and she wanted him to touch her down there. Like the first time he'd done it.

In desperation, her hands slid from his neck. Placing her palms against his muscular chest, she smiled at the way his body trembled beneath her fingertips. Tracing a line downward, she brushed over the hard muscles of his flat stomach, following the silky path of curly hair that led to the belt line of his tight pants. She struggled to unfasten the button and sighed into his hot mouth at the crisp sound as she lowered his zipper.

In a few seconds she would guide him inside her aching cunt. Oddly enough, where the idea had once frightened her, it now felt exciting and so right.

His mouth pressed harder against hers, and she enjoyed the sharp friction his chin stubble created against her mouth.

Suddenly he broke the kiss with a groan and pushed her against the countertop. Dropping his hands from her swollen, aching breasts, he gazed upon her two offerings.

"You look damn good, Sky. Damn good." His voice was thick with emotion. A faint smile lifted his passion swelled lips. "Now I wonder if you taste as good as you look."

She blinked in surprise as his head lowered. His hot tongue shot out and licked her nipple.

The warmth of his rough tongue against her tight bud startled her. Without warning he popped it into his moist mouth, making her shudder as rays of pleasure zipped through her breast.

A hand came up, clamping over her other breast. He kneaded roughly until sensual desire seared through her flesh.

He suckled her other nipple. His mouth warm, heated and wet. His tongue constantly jabbed at the tender tip, sending sexually charged messages to parts south.

His zipper forgotten, Sky reached up and ran her hands through Jim's feathery hair as he continued to suckle. Cupping the back of his head, she pulled his face into her swollen breast. This time she couldn't stifle her cry as his teeth nipped her sensitive nipple.

"Fuck me, Jim. Please fuck me."

Her words made his mouth still on her nipple, and then he pulled away.

He stared at her. Eyes dark with desire. Pupils flared with need. His breath raspy and hard.

His Adams apple bobbed as he swallowed. "I want to fuck you so bad right now it hurts. But how do I know you're ready for me? How do I know you won't say no again?"

"I won't."

His eyes widened at her answer, and she fought to inhale air as the familiar shade of hurt shone in his eyes.

He didn't believe her. He thought she was teasing him again.

Sky reached out to him but Jim backed away, his hands held up in defensive gesture as if to ward her off.

"I've got to go. They're expecting me," he said.

Turning away from her he quickly slipped out the bathroom door, closing it behind his broad back.

Dammit!

Sky stomped her foot in frustration and whirled around. Looking into the bathroom mirror, she frowned. Her bare breasts were swollen with passion. Her left nipple taut, red and aching from where Jim had suckled.

Lips bruised and passion swelled.

God, she looked pathetic. Like a foiled woman who wanted to be fucked, yet rejected by her one true love.

She'd offered herself to Jim and he'd walked away. Son of a bitch.

Sky shook her head. She had no one to blame but herself. When she saw him again, she'd make sure he understood she wanted him. Next time, she wouldn't take no for an answer.

Chapter Four

She should take a long cold shower. That would fix the problem Jim had left her with. Or maybe it wouldn't.

Visions of Jim swirled around her. Of him stepping into the shower to join her. Water sluicing off his naked body. Muscles in his arms flexing erotically as his arms reached out and his hot hands cupped her swollen breasts. Sky grabbing hold of his rigid shaft...

Sky moaned.

The pathetic sound of it ripped her back to reality.

Okay, she'd better skip the shower.

Shutting off the taps and bathroom fan, she grabbed her blouse, flicked off the lights and left the bathroom. Through the looming evening dimness that enveloped her room, she had no trouble finding the slim white package containing the vibrator.

She licked her lower lip thoughtfully. She was too wound up to be any good right now. Her skin felt too hot and too electrified. She needed to take care of business.

Within moments, Sky had slid off her shoes and her tight skirt.

The crisp white sheets sparked against her aroused nipples as she slid totally naked under the covers. She tried to ignore the pleasure the smooth linen created against her breasts, but she couldn't.

Reaching for the package containing the vibrator, Sky blew out a frustrated breath. She couldn't rip open the box and the plastic wrapped item fast enough. Thank God someone had the sense to supply the batteries. Within seconds she'd inserted the batteries and switched on the vibrator.

The low hum was music to her ears.

A smile lifted her lips and Sky closed her eyes. She didn't need to arouse her breasts, Jim had done a fine job of it.

All she needed to do was...

She gasped as the vibrator pushed past her puffy lips and rubbed against her ultra sensitive nub. Intense pleasure ripped through her cunt.

Damn that feels so good.

She moaned quietly as she rubbed the round head of the quivering machine in circular motions around her clit. The pleasure intensified. She could already feel her orgasm building.

Without hesitating, she slid the huge vibrator away and with two fingers from her other hand, slammed them against her pleasure bud where the machine had just been.

Without further adieu, she inserted the massive vibrator into her wet channel, gasping at the bliss it invoked as her cunt muscles grabbed a hold of it.

Sliding it in deeper, she couldn't help but whimper as it rammed into her maiden head.

Keeping up the strokes to her clit with one hand, she slowly, erotically slid the vibrator out again then shoved it back in. Tidal waves of sensations ripped to her very core.

Breathing hard, Sky fondled her clit. At the same time she continued her ministrations with the vibrator, using long strokes, fucking herself until her body quivered and then exploded in a mass of scorching spasms.

When it was over, Sky sighed in relief and found herself cursing Jim McBride.

That son of a bitch was dangerous. He aroused her like no other man and then he left her wanting more of him.

What was his problem anyway? Didn't he know how to fulfill a woman?

Sky shook her head in disappointment. It wasn't Jim's fault. It was her own fault. She'd teased a snake and she got bit. The vibrator had dealt with the immediate problem, but it was only a matter of time before she was aroused again.

She forced herself to focus her thoughts on the quietness sinking into the farmhouse.

Beside her bed, a cool breeze sifted through the windows caressing her hot cheeks, soothing her feverish body. She heard an owl hoot somewhere in the distance. Leaves rustled outside.

Through the layers of natural noises, she heard a sound.

An odd noise that didn't quite fit.

A creak. Like someone opening a door. Her breath caught in her lungs.

Was it her door opening? Had Jim decided to join her?

Adrenaline stabbed through her gut. Along with the surge came a kaleidoscope of physical sensations. Her heart began to hammer against her chest. Her breasts suddenly seemed larger, swollen, aching with anticipation. Her nipples tingled and throbbed at the same time.

A powerful need to be touched crawled along her skin like wildfire. Her body hummed. She knew without a doubt if Jim climbed into her bed at this very moment, she would not turn him away.

Strangely enough, the thought didn't shock her. In fact, it made her giggle in anticipation.

Tremors of want ripped through her cunt as she waited.

And waited.

No one came.

Damn!

Another creak ripped through the silence. And then another. It was followed by a low, drawn out moan.

Oh great!

Jim was having sex with one of those other women. Son of a bitch!

Throwing aside her sheets, Sky climbed out of the bed.

Reaching for her clothes, she jolted as her hands grabbed wood. Her clothes must have slipped off the night table onto the floor.

Groping through the darkness, she searched the area beside the night table but found nothing.

In the dimness, she spied the lamp and flicked the switch. Nothing happened.

Shoot! When Loverboy said lights out, he wasn't kidding.

A man's erotic groan drifted to her ears making Sky's heart pound harder.

Whoever he was it surely sounded like he was having a good time.

Opening her door, she poked her head out and listened.

The hallway seemed to come alive with sexy feminine moans. Men's erotic groans. The harsh squeak of bed springs.

Sky's pulse skittered at the seductive sounds. Her legs trembled. She found herself getting moist between her legs, yet again.

A strange banging sound captured her attention.

Was someone knocking on a door? Was someone locked in somewhere? Trying to escape? An unwilling sex slave perhaps? The missing woman?

She crept into the dark hallway. The banging sounds were coming from next door.

Tiptoeing down the hall, Sky was surprised to find the door open. Peeking inside, her heart fluttered at the sight.

Candles flickered everywhere in the room. Scented candles that gave off an exciting aroma.

Breathing deeply she pinpointed the smell as vanilla. A scent she found very arousing.

She squinted her eyes through the semi-darkness to where the banging sound came.

Oh-my-God.

A dark haired man, his back toward Sky, was thrusting madly into the petite blonde named Loren. The woman sat on some sort of workbench. Her legs clasped tight around the man's muscular hips, pressing kisses into his thick corded neck.

With every powerful thrust, the backboard banged against the wall.

Sky's cunt quivered with raw need as she imagined herself in the woman's position. Having her pussy rammed was starting to sound pretty good about now. Unfortunately she was here to do a job.

She forced herself to tear her gaze away from the two lovers. On rather shaky legs she stole down the hallway. She wondered if Loren knew she was about to be sold to a mistress. Wondered if the man fucking her was some sort of going away present for herself.

Oh boy. Those two had really been going at it. And they were enjoying themselves tremendously.

Nothing wrong with that. Nothing illegal.

By God! But the sight of those two fucking had been fantastic. The sweet ecstasy on the woman's face, wonderful.

Sky stopped short as something niggled at the back of her mind. That man. Hadn't he looked familiar?

Although she'd only seen him from the backside, hadn't he seemed similar to one of those "giggly boy" Sex Squad detectives, Jim had scolded during briefing last week?

Sky shook her head. No way. Couldn't be him.

Sighing with relief, she tiptoed further down the hallway.

She couldn't help but to stop at the next open doorway. Sky's pulse began to pound violently at the sight.

As in the other room, this one also glittered with scented candles. The aroma was different. This one smelled of roses. Romantic roses.

On the bed, legs crossed, sat four very good looking young people. Two women. Two men.

She recognized the heart shaped face woman with the auburn hair as Carmella. Loverboy's partner.

All four were completely nude, and not at all embarrassed about being that way.

God, she envied him. She wished she could be so bold. So free.

"My turn." Carmella laughed.

She drew a card from the deck between them on the bed. And smiled.

"Position 32. Climb on top of your partner and impale yourself on his rod."

Sky's pussy began to pound again.

The brunette picked the cutest guy of the two. Grinning from ear to ear, the man stretched full length on the king sized bed. His penis stuck straight up in the air.

Heavens, he was already fully aroused!

And so was Sky.

She tried to ignore the throbbing in her vagina as the woman crouched over the man and lowered herself onto his long penis. The woman grimaced as he disappeared inside her. Her loud hiss made even wore wetness cascade between Sky's legs.

Unbelievable.

They looked so natural as they watched each other get fucked. So happy.

She didn't know what she'd expected to find here in this farmhouse.

In the past, sex slaves had been slaves. Men and women held against their will. Made to perform sex for free. Maybe she'd expected to find a woman screaming as a man forced himself into her? Whips and butt plugs. A sex dungeon, maybe?

Certainly not this.

This new sex slave business looked tame. Is this another reason why the government had finally legalized sex slaves? To eradicate the horror of slavery?

But why hadn't Loverboy registered as a Sex Slave Trainer? Why was he avoiding paying his taxes? Perhaps he was deceiving these young people? Perhaps he was telling them he could provide employment so they could be trained more easily. And then when they finished their training he sold them into slavery and kept the money all to himself.

Sounded like a pretty good motive. But could she prove it?

Sky moved to the next door. It was open, too. Didn't anyone value their privacy around her?

She peeked inside. The delicate scent of magnolias filled the air as once again scented candles flickered everywhere.

This room was quiet.

Movement in a far corner caught her attention and Sky's mouth dropped open when she spotted two naked men standing in the corner.

Both had their backs toward her and Sky couldn't help but notice one of the men, the dark haired man had the curviest, sexiest ass cheeks she'd ever seen.

She found herself breathing harder when she realized it was Jim.

They were talking to each other. Their voices low, but not low enough so she couldn't make out what they were saying.

"Tonight you'll practice the trigasm on her," Loverboy said to Jim.

Trigasm? Sounded erotic.

Jim nodded. "I've studied up on it."

"Carmella said you were a quick study. I'm sure you won't disappoint your partner.

To her shock, both men suddenly turned around and spotted her.

"Ah, Sky." Loverboy seemed surprised to see her.

She didn't miss the lust flood his eyes or the way his penis swelled as he gazed hungrily upon her naked body.

Jim on the other hand looked angry. His mouth was set tight. His erection blossomed as he gazed daggers at her.

Did she detect a little jealousy in those brown eyes? Served him right.

"I'm glad to see you are eager to get into the swing of things."

Sky tried hard to act natural. To act as if this wasn't her first time standing totally naked in front of two men. She focused her mind on the four men and women she'd seen earlier sitting cross-legged on the bed. Focused on how casual they acted in the nude.

Sweet mercy, as hard as she tried, she couldn't keep her face from heating up at both their hungry stares. She wished the floor would simply engulf her.

"There's that virgin blush, again." Loverboy cooed.

Beside him, Jim stiffened and quickly came to her rescue. She shivered at his icy tone. "This must be my partner. The one you were talking about."

"Go easy on her. She's unsure whether she wants to become a sex slave. Give her a real good time, though."

"I intend on doing just that." Jim's eyes bored straight into hers and she looked away.

"I'll be going." Loverboy said. "I have a few more students to check on. I'll pop in once in a while to see how things are going in here. If you'll excuse me."

When Loverboy left the room, Sky stood paralyzed as Jim's fierce gaze captured her. His mouth looked absolutely delicious as those sexy lips of his tilted upward.

A wonderful expanse of shoulders flowed out to bulging muscles in his arms. Muscles ridged his narrow belly and abdomen. Tufts of dark hair grew across his broad chest and arrowed down....

Oh my!

He was extremely... well endowed and very... aroused.

Sky couldn't help but stare.

A few heartbeats of silence followed. Then he started to walk toward her. His hard balls swaying with his stride. His massive penis quite erect.

She couldn't seem to keep her eyes off... it.

The anticipation of actually have it buried inside her cunt made a low moan escape her lips.

Sky took a deep breath, drawing the warm scented air into her lungs. She tried to relax.

Couldn't.

Tried to think. Couldn't do that either.

God, Jim's penis was so huge.

Arousal coursed through her veins, weakening her, urging her to reach out to him...

She should stay away from him. Oh God! He looked so good without clothes.

Her breasts swelled with pride as his hot gaze raked across her body.

Oh shit! She was in big trouble. Big trouble.

"If I hadn't been here that bastard would be fucking you right now." He spat as he brushed past her.

"Any objections?" she teased.

He swore beneath his breath, shutting the door. A little too loudly, she might add.

He whirled around to face her.

"Jesus! Why the hell are you walking around like this? You're just begging for a man to fuck you, aren't you?"

"I thought you said I would be the one who couldn't handle this?"

He blinked at her as if she'd just slapped him.

"I can handle it, if you can." His voice was now a deadly calm. She didn't miss the note of challenge.

"Lay down on the bed. On your back. With your ass near the edge. Lift you knees up. Feet on the mattress. Spread your legs. You're about to be taught a lesson." His voice was hard, angry.

"Another finger fucking?"

"How'd you know?"

Her breath hitched in her lungs at his answer.

Sweet heavens, how far were they going to take this? They were supposed to be looking for the missing woman. But they were also supposed to participate in the lessons, if necessary.

And by the way the excitement was building in her body, this lesson was necessary.

The blood shot wildly in her veins as she slowly lay on the bed and did as he told her. When she lifted her knees up and spread her legs, he walked toward her.

She swallowed. His brown eyes were intense. His gaze hungry as those eyes raked up and down her body, finally settling on her cunt.

"Tonight's lesson is the trigasm," he said thickly.

Her breathing grew deeper, her breasts rising and falling in a sensuous rhythm. Her nipples had never felt so tight. So aching with need.

She inhaled sharply as his thick muscled arms reached out. His hands branded her inner thighs as he pried her trembling legs open wider for his inspection. His masculine aroma reached her nostrils, the intoxicating scent sending her heartbeat soaring.

"A trigasm can be achieved by vigorously massaging the three points of pleasure." The anger was slowly leaving his voice, replaced by a sensuous tone.

"And what would those three be?" she whispered, her gaze suddenly obsessed with the look of need shining in his eyes.

His right hand slid slowly along her inner thigh leaving a trail of tingling heat. His hot fingers peeled her nether lips apart. His eyes widened with appreciation as he studied her cunt. And then the tips of his lips curved upward in a satisfying smile.

Sky's heart beat harder.

When his thick thumb pushed against her clit, she inhaled a moan. He began to move his thumb over her sensitive nub in small, slow torturous circles, making her ache.

"Number One pleasure point is the clitoris," he rumbled. His thumb moving sensuously, his full lips now tight with concentration.

She could hear the wet sounds of her cunt juice as his fingers dipped inside her vagina ever so slightly and came out again in a teasing promise of things to come. The moistness between her legs grew. His pace quickened. The pressure against her pleasure nub increased.

Sky closed her eyes tightly as the whirlwinds of pleasure ripped through her.

Sweet, sweet torture.

His thumb kept the pressure on as it swirled against her pleasure nub. She cried out when a couple of his fingers slipped into her hot channel. About an inch inside, he pressed a finger against the wall of her vagina. Sky inhaled sharply at the gesture.

"Number two is the g-spot." Jim murmured. "It is the spongy area that can be felt through the front wall of the vagina."

"G-spot? I heard it was a myth," she gasped.

"Not so. It exists. I'll prove it to you."

Sky's breathing intensified as the pressure of his fingers increased as he searched along her vaginal wall. His thumb continued to rub against her pleasure nub.

Sky closed her eyes tighter, the tension in her body mounted. Her fingers drew to her swollen breasts and she began to knead herself. To pinch her nipples until they screamed with aches.

She threw her head back and allowed the sweet torture to rule her body.

"The size and sensitivity of g-spots differ in women. So I have to experiment. In order to find it, I can use the come-hither technique. It means I wave my finger." Jim's husky voice came from somewhere far away. She felt his finger move slightly and Sky jerked as he touched a sensitive spot in her cunt. A stream of wetness dripped down her ass.

"Here it is. The key is keep you aroused. Keep the touch firm."

As promised, he increased the pressure on her g-spot. Wetness poured from her vagina. Her thighs trembled uncontrollably under his onslaught. His movements against her clit exquisite agony. His free hand left her inner thigh and a finger slurped against her moisture, spreading it lower, slowly heading toward her other hole.

She bucked as a large finger dipped inside her anal canal. The sensation was strange. Filling. Then his finger quickly popped out.

It moved back up, collecting more moisture and then dipped back down and in. Just a little further each time.

Sky shuddered at the intimate gesture.

"Third area for a trigasm is the anus."

Oh God! Her hips instinctively arched higher, allowing him easier access to her.

Her cunt felt like an inferno. She wanted him to mount her. To plunge into her. To quench this insane fire raging throughout her body.

"Clitoris. G Spot. Anus." He whispered. His finger movements were now sensual and in perfect rhythm. She couldn't take it anymore. She needed release. Now!

"Jim! Please!"

"What?"

"Fuck me!" she gasped.

"I can't do that, Sky. Remember? You wanted to remain a virgin until we're married."

Disappointment ripped along the excruciating sensations. She was going to go insane if he didn't finish this.

"Please," she begged.

His finger in her anus speared deeper. The fingers in her cunt began to thrust hard. It was coming. She could feel it. She whimpered with excitement.

"Faster! Oh God! Faster!"

The fingers impaling her thrust harder. Became more violent. More frantic.

The pressure built to intolerable pleasure.

Sky screamed. Hard and loud. She didn't care who heard her. Didn't care about anything except for the way her body convulsed with the sharp blades of spasms as the release she ached for imploded.

Chapter Five

Sky lay naked and willing in front of him. Her breasts heaved sensuously as she breathed wildly from the trigasm that had convulsed her body. Her cunt lay splayed wide open for him to enter. And boy did he want to enter. To bury his steel rod into her hot tight hole.

And yet, he couldn't do it.

Up until now, she'd stuck to her principles. She'd wanted to remain a virgin until she got married.

Shit! He wanted her so fucking bad his rod throbbed. But it wasn't fair to take her when she was so goddamn vulnerable.

For his saintly efforts of restraint, Jim had himself the worst hard on he'd ever had in his entire life.

Suddenly she opened her eyes. They were a deep blue. A pretty blue. They glittered with love as she looked up at him.

His heart twisted. He saw the turmoil in her eyes. The want for more sex. The need for his love. And he needed her in his life, too.

The realization made him curse softly.

Slowly her blue eyes widened as her gaze lowered to his impressive erection. That sweet pink tongue popped out of her wet mouth as she thoughtfully licked her bottom lip.

Then she smiled. It was a challenging smile. And it made Jim wonder what the hell she was up to now.

She sat up. Her naked breasts jiggled as she scrambled on her hands and knees on the bed toward him. Her face came level with his upturned rod.

Sweet Jesus! Was she about to do what he hoped?

His hard penis pulsed with need as she stared at it. Her beautiful face serene.

She opened her mouth and her moist, velvety lips curled around the tip of his hard cock.

Damn! The inexperienced way her mouth tightened around him made the need in his penis mount to a painful level. His legs staggered beneath him, and he curled his hands around her shoulders to steady himself.

"Suck!" He groaned.

Through half lidded eyes, he watched as her cheeks hollowed out and she sucked. Hard.

Shards of lightning ripped through his shaft, slamming his balls and right into his gut.

Her tongue dipped and moved sensuously against the underneath part of the head of his shaft. The gesture made him cry out at the pleasurable sensations cascading up and down his trembling length.

He could feel himself tighten as her tongue slithered around his head. His breathing became labored. Raspy. The heat of her moist mouth clamped around his rod felt good. So damn good.

How the hell could her innocent probing turn him on so much? He hadn't felt like this with even the most experienced women he'd been with.

Her lips loosened slightly, and she took more of him in. Her mouth worked in slow, torturous movements that left him gasping.

He groaned when her hot hands came up and covered his balls. The intimate gesture almost brought him to his knees. Her fingers explored his scrotum area, making him groan. His hips automatically thrust forward, slamming his penis deeper into her mouth.

Somewhere at the back of his mind, he wondered if maybe she was frightened as his hips began to gyrate. But his concerns were immediately put to rest when her tongue seductively circled his stiff rod, sending incredible jolts ripping through his shaft.

He couldn't help but to thrust into her mouth. Her lips stretched tight over his flesh. Her mouth was a hot cavern. So goddamn hot and moist.

His thrusting increased. A moan slipped from her mouth. To his surprise she took him in deeper.

Her fingers were stroking his balls now. Stroking and kneading. The pressure inside his penis grew to an intolerable level. He could feel the hot spiral of his orgasm coming.

"Sky!" He gasped in warning. "I'm going to come!"

Her tongue began to lick the tip of his penis, encouraging him to spew. His hips began to thrust uncontrollably.

He sunk his hands into her short feathery hair. Grabbed the back of her head, pulled her face against him.

He thrust harder. Violently. A frenzy of sensations convulsed through his shaft.

Her moist mouth suckled his fiery flesh. His breath caught in his lungs. His body tightened erotically and then he couldn't hold back anymore.

He cried out as he ejaculated. Hot seed spewed into her mouth like a geyser. His body shuddered against her face. The release was magnificent. Absolutely fantastic.

The feel of her hot tight mouth was excruciating as she continued to suck hard, dragging his seed from him until he was dry and shuddering under her onslaught.

When she let go of him, he slumped onto his knees, totally satiated. Totally wiped out.

They stared at each other for a long time. Their gazes clashing as they breathed heavily. Suddenly Sky's eyes darkened again. Darkened with desire.

Christ! She wanted him to give her another trigasm.

"Nice to see you two getting so acquainted." Loverboy's amused voice curled through the candle lit room.

Jim looked up to find Loverboy hovering behind Sky. A cocky grin on his goddamn face. His lust filled eyes caressed Sky's bare ass.

Jim tensed and fought wildly against the urge to cover Sky's naked body from Loverboy's hungry gaze.

Christ! They'd been so enthralled with each other, they hadn't even heard Loverboy enter the room.

And now he stood behind Sky, his massive rod mere inches from her velvety ass. He noticed Sky tense as Loverboy ran a long finger along her smooth backside.

Jim was about to tell him to get his dirty hands off his woman when Sky shot him a warning look.

"Well, Sky? How was the trigasm? Did Jim do a fine job?"

To Jim's surprise, the fear vanished from her face and her lips upturned into a delightful smile.

"He was absolutely wonderful. Where do I sign up for this sex slave course?"

Her words stunned Jim. And her next action stunned him even further.

Slowly, seductively she sat down on her ass and crossed her legs exposing her delicious cunt and her breasts to Loverboy. Loverboy didn't waste any time drooling over the fantastic sight she was exposing him to.

The urge to slam his fist into Loverboy's nose was so strong, Jim physically had to bite his tongue. It was only when he drew blood from where his teeth sunk into his flesh that he felt the pain push aside some of his anger.

He didn't miss the pulse in Sky's throat quicken when her gaze latched onto Loverboy's naked physique. Onto his vein riddled penis. The man had a hard on the size of a massive cucumber and he wore it proudly. Too goddamn proudly.

Jealousy ripped through him and he bit back a curse.

"I'd like to speak some more to you about this course. In private. If that's all right?" she asked Loverboy.

"I can give you all the details in my office. Then there is a contract to sign."

"If I like what I hear, I'll be more than willing to sign the contract."

Loverboy nodded his head in satisfaction.

"How about I show you to my office?"

Jim tensed as he awaited her answer.

"I feel business should be business and pleasure should be pleasure," Sky said. "And since your office is a business environment, I'd appreciate the return of my clothes."

Relief swept over Jim at her words. But Loverboy didn't like her demand. The thought of covering up Sky's luscious body from his prying eyes, seemed to make Loverboy's erection shrink ever so slightly.

Good! That prick didn't deserve to gaze upon Sky the way he was doing. Didn't deserve to even look at her with her clothes on, let alone off.

Christ! Why the hell hadn't he just kidnapped Sky after she'd taken this assignment. He should have stashed her somewhere safe. Where no other man could look at her nakedness. No man except him.

"Very well, Sky." Loverboy broke into his thoughts. "You are correct. Business should be business. Your clothes are in this closet." He pointed to a nearby door. His gaze turned to Jim. "Jim, would you mind showing Sky to my office?"

"No problem." Jim nodded.

"I'll see you downstairs in a few minutes," Loverboy said.

When Loverboy had once again left the room, Sky breathed a sigh of relief.

The sound of her breath escaping her lungs brought little relief to him.

"That bastard!" Jim cursed as he headed for the closet.

Flinging it open, he withdrew her flimsy blouse and the sexy tight leather skirt.

"Where's your goddamn underwear?" He asked when his searching showed up nothing.

"I didn't wear any."

"You didn't! Holy Christ, woman. What are you thinking?"

"Sexy is what I'm thinking, Jim. That is the whole point in trying to get Loverboy's attention, remember?"

She grabbed her clothes from him.

He watched in stunned fascination as she lifted her long legs and stepped into that tight skirt, effectively concealing her pussy from his hot gaze. Her luscious breasts bounced wildly as she began to slip on the blouse.

He could feel his penis tightening again.

"What are you going to do inside the office? Just the two of you?"

"That green head of jealousy is popping up." She grinned as she slid her blouse over her shoulders.

"It's my other head that wants to pop into you." he warned crisply.

Before she could hide her breasts from his hungry gaze, he reached out and grabbed her wrists, stopping her cold.

Suddenly, he wanted to taste her breasts again. Wanted to suckle her sweet nipples. Wanted to feel her softness press against his face.

Obviously she read the intent in his eyes, because she tried to cover herself.

"No, don't. I want to look at you," he said, his hungry gaze raking her luscious breasts.

"Jim, he's downstairs waiting."

"I don't goddamn care. You're mine. You belong to me. You hear me?"

The look of surprise on her face just about did him in. Didn't she know how much he wanted her? Didn't she know he was a stupid jerk for breaking their engagement?

"It's over between us, Jim. You said so yourself. You couldn't wait." Her softly spoken words slammed into his gut and he almost doubled over from the impact.

"I lied. I can wait." The truth of his words made her inhale sharply. "Don't let him touch you, Sky."

"I won't."

"Promise me."

"Trust me," she whispered. The warmth from her breath caressed his lips erotically. He wanted a taste of those lips. Just one quick taste. He felt his head begin to lower to her mouth.

Her hot hands slammed against his chest, stopping him cold.

"I have to go. Where's his office?"

Shit!

"Down the stairs. Turn left through the living room. The door beside the television set. I haven't been able to search it yet."

"I'll see what I can do. While I'm in there, you look around for Sally. Or try to find out where she is."

Jim nodded. It was time to put sex aside. Reluctantly, he released her and watched her button up her blouse with trembling fingers.

"Don't know why you wore that flimsy thing. It leaves nothing to my imagination," he grumbled as he stared at her dark nipples popping seductively against the white material.

"That's the idea." She winked and slipped out the door.

* * * *

You're mine! You belong to me!

Jim's words rang through Sky's head as she tiptoed barefoot down the stairs.

Was Jim serious? Or was it just his sex crazed mind talking?

Did she dare to hope they'd get back together? If what they'd just shared was any indication how good they would be in bed...

Sky blew out a hot breath as she remembered the way his touch had ripped apart her body. How he'd turned her into a moaning, writhing bundle of joy.

She wanted more of that pleasure. Wanted all of Jim. But first she needed to do her job. Then they could get out of here. Talk things over like two civilized adults. Maybe pick up their plans of getting married again?

The door to Loverboy's office stood open and light streamed out into the dark living room. No sound came from the office.

Peeking inside, she was glad to see the small room empty. Popping inside she quietly closed the door.

Turning around, she surveyed the room. It was a typical office. A desk flooded with papers. A couple of swivel chairs. A filing cabinet.

Sky immediately headed for the filing cabinet. If the missing woman had come back to Loverboy willingly she might have signed a contract.

As quietly as possible she slid open the top drawer and surveyed the folders. Accounts Payable. Bills. Expenses. Nothing giving any indication of contracts.

She slid open the second drawer and smiled. Bingo! Names. The Chief's daughter's last name was Green. In a flash, she sifted to the G section and found what she was looking for.

A contract in the name Sally Anne Green. She'd been sold to a man living in Alaska for $300,000 dollars. The contract wasn't signed. Sky's heart picked up speed.

$300,000? Very interesting. A far cry from the $100,000 she'd mentioned to the police.

What did the unsigned contract mean? Had Sally been forced into slavery?

A sound from outside the door caught her attention. Dropping the contract back into the folder, she quickly slid the drawer shut and plopped into the nearest chair.

A split second later the door swung open and Loverboy walked in. Thankfully he was dressed in a white shirt and casual slacks.

Sky exhaled in relief. If he'd shown up naked expecting to her to perform on him, she would have died on the spot.

"I'm sorry to keep you waiting. I had to attend to some pleasure."

Ookay.

"Now! Let me explain how our sex slave classes work." He sat down on the chair behind his desk and clasped his hands behind his head, looking totally relaxed.

She wished she could relax, unfortunately, all she could think about was Jim and praying he would be careful.

"As I was saying, your pay would be $100,000 a year. You would be expected to perform any sexual duties your master or mistress asks. Including performing on any of his or her friends. Would you be comfortable with that?"

"Performing on someone other than my master?"

Loverboy nodded.

"I would have to obey my master, wouldn't I? His word would be my command regardless of whether I like it." Damned if she would sleep with any other man than Jim.

"During my training course, you will be exposed to all the basics of what a master or mistress will demand from you. It is the best way to sensitize yourself to your new world. There will be classes in oral sex, anal sex, threesomes, different positions, and many more exciting courses. The last week would be in the Sex Dungeon."

"What's that?"

Loverboy unclasped his hand from behind his head and leaned forward. Excitement gleamed in his eyes.

"Your final week is spent in the Sex Dungeon where you are forced to put into practice what you've learned here. We have potential masters and mistresses who come and try you out."

Mercy. This slave business wasn't as easy as she'd thought earlier tonight.

"The masters and mistresses experiment with the students in the Dungeon. It gives both the potential owner and slave an idea if they are compatible."

"What a unique idea," Sky forced herself to say.

"I thought so too when my partner came up with the idea. Oh and before I forget to mention it, the Sex Dungeon is also available to all the Sex Slave students, past, present or future who attend my course. You are free to go downstairs anytime to try out the male or female we have down there. It gives the students an idea of what will happen to them when they leave here. As a matter of fact that's where I just came from." He grinned. "Seeing your beautiful naked pussy all wet from your encounters with Jim gave me one hell of a hard on."

Sky tried hard not to stiffen at his words. Tried hard not to shiver as she imagined herself locked away in a dungeon being forced to have sex with Loverboy or a stranger.

"I wouldn't mind having a tour of the Sex Dungeon."

"What a wonderful idea. But first let's discuss the contract, shall we?"

Oh yes, the contract.

He slid a desk drawer open, withdrew a paper and placed it onto a cleared area on his desk.

"It is a standard form. The contract explains more in detail of what would be expected from you and the courses you would take. Of course, before you sign the contract I would have to give you a physical."

Sky froze. She could feel cold perspiration dot her forehead.

"A physical?"

"To see if you are healthy. Blood tests for sexual diseases. Internal exam. Routine stuff."

Internal exam? Oh God! How the hell was she going to get out of this one?

"Since you are so eager, we can do it right now. I have an adjoining room where I do the physical, draw the blood, get the urine. I send the items to the lab and I'll have the results in twenty-four hours. Then you can sign the contract."

Sky's heart thumped loudly in her ears. The thought of Loverboy's hands touching her body made her feel sick. But what else could she do? The last thing she needed was to make him suspicious by denying his request. Sky drew in a ragged breath and nodded in agreement.

Chapter Six

Red hot anger ripped through Jim as he gazed down at the woman lying naked on the bed.

He'd found her.

He'd found Sally Green. And she was drugged up to her eyeballs.

She'd grown into quite the woman since the last time he'd seen her three or four years ago. Back then she'd been in pig tails, wearing braces and tomboyish when she'd opened the door to her home. She'd said nothing to him as she'd quickly accepted the files his boss had requested for Jim to bring over while his boss recovered from gallbladder surgery. Then she'd slammed the door shut in his face.

Now Sally was long legged and very curvy. A natural beauty.

Her waist length blond hair was tangled with perspiration. Her face chalk white. Full breasts rose and fell as she breathed heavily.

Her long legs were spread eagle. Her shaven cunt exposed and wet with semen. Her eyes were wide open. Fixed as she stared straight through him.

He closed his eyes against the sickening sight, remembering how only minutes ago he had seen Loverboy come through the secret door in the kitchen.

Jim had been surprised to see the kitchen wall move. Only his quick thinking had enabled him to slip undetected into the nearby broom closet.

Through the crack in the slightly open door, he'd watched him turn the thermostat one full turn and saw the door swing shut.

Christ! He wouldn't have believed it if he hadn't seen it. A secret door to an underground passage that led to several locked rooms.

This one had been the only one unlocked. Obviously Loverboy had been in too much of a hurry to get to his meeting with Sky.

Sally moaned. Her lashes fluttered and her sightless eyes closed.

Jim picked up her limp arm. Her skin felt clammy and cool as he pressed two fingers against her wrist.

Her pulse was strong but slow.

"Sally? Sally? Can you hear me?"

"Loverboy? You back so soon? You just can't get enough of me, can you?"

She opened her eyes and giggled. Her fingers reached up and ran smoothly along his jaw line. She smiled seductively.

"What did they give you, Sally? Do you know?"

Her brows pressed together in a frown. "Sex drugs. It's part of the course. You should know that." She blinked wildly trying to focus. "Who are you? You're not Loverboy."

"I'm a student here."

"Sent down to fuck me?"

Jim's eyes moved to her rising breasts as she inhaled deeply. Her arms reached out, grabbing him around his waist.

"Do with me what you want. Your wish is my command, master," she said as she looked up at him. Her head lolled sideways like a rag doll. She giggled again.

Jim scanned the bare room looking for her clothing. He saw nothing. Not even a goddamn bed sheet to cover her nakedness.

"I'm here to get you out, Sally."

"I'm not leaving here. I'm almost finished with my course." Her smile widened. "I'm pretty sure that big black man will take me. He seemed to have no trouble sticking his big pecker into my tight hole. I told Loverboy I want him. Or maybe I'll take you. You're cute."

Her grasp around his waist tightened.

To his shock she pressed a hot kiss against the head of his semi-erect penis.

Jesus. He had to get her out of here. Fast.

"Sorry Sally, I'm already taken."

"I should have known Loverboy would find someone for you. How come I haven't seen you here before?" Her eyes narrowed with curiosity. "Haven't we met before?"

"I'm new." No use telling her who he was. She'd figure it out soon enough.

"New? And you already have a mistress?"

"A girlfriend. Now c'mon, let's get you out of here. Your father is worried about you."

Sally blinked in puzzlement, then laughed.

"My father? Worried about me? Hell, he probably misses fucking me."

Jim's closed his eyes and cursed.

"Oh! Didn't daddy dearest tell you? I've been his sex toy since I was eight. I refuse to do it for free anymore. Tell my father he can go fuck himself! I'm not going back to him."

Great! Just great! What the hell was he supposed to do now? Believe what she was telling him? It could be the drugs talking. But the look of pain in her eyes made him believe she was telling the truth.

Should he still get her out of here? Or leave her to her fate?

"Why'd you go to the cops then?" he asked.

"I never went to the goddamn authorities. My father made it up when I told him I wanted to be a sex slave. My only mistake was throwing it in his face that I was being trained by Loverboy."

Jim inhaled in frustration. This was just great. This whole assignment was just a ruse? A con job thought up by a jilted father.

Shit! If he didn't bring Sally Green back to the bastard, he'd probably make Jim lose his job.

He looked down at Sally. At the way her eyes were fixed because of the sex drugs. Drugs that she was fully aware of and fully accepting.

Who the hell was he to make the decision of what Sally Green should do anyway? She was sixteen. Legal age to do whatever she wanted.

Suddenly a faint puff of alluring perfume sunk a warning deep into Jim's lungs. He recognized the scent and his blood stalled in his veins.

Carmella's perfume.

Sally's grip around his waist tightened.

He heard movement from behind him.

Before he could wrench himself from Sally's hold and turn around, pain exploded like a bomb against the right side of his head.

The impact stunned him. He toppled over, hitting the ground, hard.

Bright white stars blinded his vision.

He blinked.

The stars remained.

Shit!

He'd been hit real good. He couldn't move. He was screwed.

Someone kicked at his legs. He wanted to kick back. Nothing happened.

Rough hands grabbed his naked shoulder and rolled him onto his back. The stars danced wildly, making him nauseous. That alluring perfume drove deep into his lungs.

Warm feminine fingers roughly groped his testicles and then slid over his penis.

Fingers searched. Squeezed. Kneaded.

Despite his grogginess he found himself hardening under her harsh exploration. Finally, she let go of his privates, and he exhaled a shuddering breath.

"He's the undercover cop I was telling you about. Want me to kill him?" The man's voice was unmistakable. He was one of his own hand picked Sex Squad detectives. A man with a perfect record who'd asked for a position on the Squad. One of the two men who hadn't taken the Loverboy case seriously enough during Briefing last week. Or at least, Jim had thought he hadn't taken it seriously. Apparently he had, because here he was.

"No, Loverboy wants him alive."

Someone lifted his feet. Hands slid under his armpits. He felt himself being lifted. Felt his head whirl violently. Before he passed out he could only think of Sky, and hoped to God Loverboy wouldn't fuck her into being a sex slave.

* * * *

"Sky. There's no need to be frightened," Loverboy drawled.

Damn, he could see right through her.

"It's just a physical. I won't hurt you. I just need to feel around inside. It's the same as a pap smear."

"I'm not afraid," she said as she slid off the cot he'd instructed her to sit on. "I guess I'm a little shy. I need just a little more time. A day or two."

Loverboy frowned. "You didn't seem shy with Jim."

"Oh, well, he's a fellow student." Lame excuse.

"Meaning?"

Her cheeks began to burn with embarrassment.

"I'm attracted to you. It wouldn't be professional. I'd enjoy your touch," she lied. Sickness clawed at her belly.

"All the more why I should touch you, Sky. I can pleasure you in ways you've never dreamed of."

He started toward her.

Oh dear. She was in trouble here. Jim, where the hell are you?

"I thought you didn't do virgins?" she stammered.

"I lied."

Big news flash there.

"Virgins are my weakness," Loverboy cooed as he slowly trailed her. His eyes burned with lust.

"How's that?" she asked as she circled behind his desk, stalling for time. If she could keep him talking she might be able to get to the door.

"My upbringing. The nuns were virgins until I serviced them."

Sky blinked in disbelief. "You fucked nuns?"

"They fucked me." Anger coiled in his voice. "In the orphanage. I protested at first. But they were women. Lonely women. Bigger than me. Stronger. I found out quickly they were sensuous creatures who only wanted to be loved. God didn't mean for them to be locked away in a convent without the love of a man. So, they used us orphanage boys. I serviced the nuns for years. Even while I was a preacher. I learned to look for the yearning in their eyes. But you're different, Sky. I saw the yearning in your eyes. The yearning for a man you'd lost. He hurt you so bad. He made you vulnerable. Despite that fact, there's a strength in you I just can't help but to try to dominate. I couldn't leave you in that bar to get fucked by some stranger. I want you all to myself."

"If you love to fuck women, why bother becoming a preacher?"

His eyes glazed over with remembrance. Sky poised herself, ready to run for the door.

"I did it for the nuns. They thought if I became a preacher I'd stay with them. I would be able to satisfy their lust."

"And you could forgive them for their carnal sins during confession? I bet they thought you would be the closest thing to making love to God, am I right?"

His eyes twinkled with amusement.

"Never thought about the God part, but yes. I think you're right."

Sky leaped for the door. Her back prickled in warning, and she screamed as Loverboy's strong hands curled around her waist.

* * * *

Jim's head hurt like a son of a bitch.

Last thing he remembered was Sally Green holding him around his waist. And Carmella's perfume. Then excruciating pain as someone bashed him over the head.

At that memory, Jim's eyes flew open in alarm.

Directly above him a thick beamed ceiling with a lit bare light bulb rolled into view. The air smelled musty. Damp.

Obviously they'd dumped him in one of those other locked rooms in the basement of the farmhouse.

He tried to turn his head to get a better view of his surroundings, but the secure band strapped over his forehead prevented movement.

A tinge of panic hummed along his nerves. He smelled leather.

Leather restraints.

One across his forehead. Another velvety strap pinned down his neck.

He tested his arms. They were outstretched at ninety degree angles. Restraints pinned his elbows and his wrists. He wiggled his fingers. At least something was free. It gave him a glimmer of hope.

Mentally he checked the rest of his body. His legs were spread-eagle. Bands were lashed over his knees and ankles.

Everything was secure.

Except for his groin area.

He lifted his hips up and then down, gasping at the sharp needle pricks of pain biting into his ass cheeks.

What the hell?

He repeated the maneuver.

When he lowered his ass, this time ever so gently, the same thing happened.

Ouch.

Okay. So he was supposed to keep his ass still. He could do that. For now.

A wave of confusion mixed with fear tumbled over him as he suddenly realized he was totally defenseless.

And totally naked.

Great. Just great.

He groaned at the memory of Carmella groping his balls and penis before he'd passed out. The bitch had known exactly where to touch in order to arouse him.

What the hell did they plan on doing to him down here? Were they going to turn him into one of those sex slaves? Pump drugs into him like they'd done to Sally Green?

Making love to strange women wasn't his cup of tea. He wanted only one. Sky. And now that he'd experienced the sexual side of her, he wanted her in his life even more.

A soft sexy moan drifted to his ears. A woman's aroused moan. Whoever she was sounded like she was enjoying herself.

He heard a man grunt.

The light bulb overhead swayed slightly. The far-off sounds of springs creaking made Jim's pulse begin to hammer.

Was the moaning woman, Sky? Was Loverboy fucking her?

The moans grew louder. Didn't sound like her. Sky's moans had been distinct. Sweet and sexy and innocent.

This had to be someone else. Probably his kidnappers.

Jim rolled his eyes.

Christ! His kidnappers were having sex right over his head. More grunts and moans followed. Whoever was up there was certainly going at it. Good and hard.

Jim's breathing quickened at the tantalizing sounds. He imagined himself leaning over a naked Sky.

Her legs wide open. His rod hard and stiff, eager to dip into her wet cunt.

At the vision, Jim felt himself go hard. His cock swelled. Rose to the occasion.

An erotic scream ripped through the stillness. Then everything went completely silent.

Shit! Don't stop now!

Not when his cock was standing at attention and as hard as a goddamn rock.

He heard the stairs creak. Someone was coming.

Panic stole his breath. His penis dropped dead from fright. He winced at the sound of a heavy bolt screeching across a metal door. A key grated in the lock.

Jesus! The way they had him trussed up like a Thanksgiving turkey and held under lock and key meant they didn't want him going anywhere.

His heart cracked against his chest like a battering ram as the door opened. Footsteps entered the room. He heard someone breathing.

Carmella hovered into view. Shit! He couldn't deny she was a beautiful woman. He'd had a hell of time getting her attention when he'd started to frequent the Sexy Toys Shop she owned. One week wasn't too much time to capture her attention and get invited to the Sex Slave Course. But he'd been lucky, especially when she'd asked him to perform oral sex on her in the back room of the Shop. Back then he'd been desperate. Sky had accepted the assignment and he would have done anything to get into the farmhouse as her backup.

Carmella's wide spaced dark brown eyes blinked down at him. Soft auburn curls caressed her heart shaped face. Her full mouth pouted sexily.

"I'm glad to see I didn't hit you too hard." Her voice sounded soft and delicate and deadly.

He couldn't help but flinch as her soft fingers caressed what he suspected was a goose egg sized lump just above his temple where the pain radiated.

"I see I hit you a little too hard. I do apologize, Jim."

"What's the big idea strapping me down like this, Carmella?"

"Just relax. Let me massage away your headache."

He was about to protest when her fingers began massaging his temple with tiny, gentle soothing circles.

The pain began to ebb almost immediately. Obviously she was an expert on whacking people and bringing relief.

Despite the tenseness of the situation, he found himself relaxing under her ministrations. With the relaxation came curiosity.

His gaze dropped from her pretty face and followed the slender column of her neck to the curve of her shoulder.

A very naked shoulder with a dusting of rust colored freckles. He followed the trail of freckles down to…

Holy shit!

She was naked.

Not good.

Two very large breasts jiggled not too far away from his mouth. Dusky rose nipples poked straight out at him as if to say, here I am, have yourself a taste.

He swallowed nervously. He didn't know why he should be so surprised to see her naked. It wasn't as if he hadn't seen Carmella naked earlier tonight as he'd watched her entertain the students during tonight's lessons.

"What do you want, Carmella?"

Perhaps he shouldn't have asked. The tip of her tongue peeked through her luscious mouth and her hopeful gaze raked down to his penis. "You are very well endowed."

"I've no complaints so far."

"Most women say size matters. I tend to agree with them, but the man must know what to do in order to bring about the utmost pleasure in a woman."

Jim narrowed his eyes with suspicion. "Exactly what kind of game are you playing?"

"Curious mia cara? That's wonderful. It means you're open to new and exciting things."

"Listen, if you're looking for a fascinating fuck, I can oblige you. Just untie me." Then I'll leave, he added silently. There was no way he'd let this woman introduce him to "new and exciting." He'd be betraying Sky if he did.

"I don't want to untie you, darling. I prefer a… captive audience."

Lust sparkled in her eyes. Shit! He needed to get out of here. Pronto.

"Carmella? What are you planning to do to me?"

"Please don't be frightened, Jim."

A shiver of fear crawled up his spine. Past experience had taught him to be scared when someone told him not to be.

Jim's breath caught as her warm fingertips pressed delicately against the middle of his mouth, quieting him.

"Shh." Her finger began to massage the left corner of his mouth. Soothing little circles like she'd done to his temple.

Slowly. Gently. Erotically.

Shit. The corner of his mouth was beginning to loosen.

She switched to the other side. Massaging until the tightness of his skin around his lips evaporated.

"It won't work."

"What won't work, darling?"

"Whatever you are trying to get me to do. It just won't work."

"What is it I'm trying to do?" she asked sweetly.

"You're trying to seduce my mouth into doing something for you. I'm not playing your games, Carmella. I'm a new student here. I haven't been introduced to all the new exciting things yet. Why don't we wait until I'm more… experienced?"

"You already seem so experienced, Jim. I thoroughly enjoyed your performance at the back of my store."

Guilt ripped through his gut. She'd enjoyed herself. He hadn't. And he sure as hell wasn't enjoying himself now. What he needed to do was find out exactly how much the other detective had told her about Sky.

"Quit the crap, Carmella. I know you know who I am."

She pouted. "Oh pooh, you Sex Squad detectives need so much work in loosening you up. I can see you aren't interested in playing with me tonight. But there is something I have to tell you before I release you…."

Jim frowned. He didn't like the coolness in her voice. Instinctively, he knew she was about to tell him something he wasn't going to like.

* * * *

"Don't be frightened, Sky," Loverboy said as she struggled in his arms.

"Frightened? Me?" She tried to laugh. Couldn't. "I'll show you how scared I am. Would you care to join me in my bedroom?" Hopefully at the invitation, Loverboy would let go of her and she could escape.

To her relief his hands loosened slightly around her waist.

"I'd prefer to do you right here, Sky. Right here on the cot. Except I won't do you with my fingers, like Jim did at Sex Squad Headquarters."

Sky froze.

"Oh come on! Don't look so surprised, Sky O'Kelley, Sex Squad Detective. You honestly think I don't keep track of my incoming virgins?"

"You better be careful, Loverboy," Sky warned. "I am a government agent. People know I'm here. It can get quite sticky if I should disappear."

"Oh Sky, ye of little faith. Nothing's going to happen to you. That is, nothing that you don't want to happen."

Sky swallowed, her throat suddenly going dry.

"What do you mean?"

"It means we're going up to your room, Sky."

Fear grabbed hold of her. There was no way in hell she was going to have sex with Loverboy. No way in hell!

On the other hand.... The cuffs! She had handcuffs in her purse. The purse was in her room. But she didn't remember seeing it when she searched for her clothes. Panic welled again.

No! Wait a minute. She'd left her purse in the bathroom. By the sink. They might have missed it when they'd taken her clothes.

"Let's head up to your room, Sky. Nice and slow. No funny moves."

His arm stayed snug around her waist as he led her from his office. They entered the dark living room. Frantically she searched for Jim. He was nowhere in sight.

As they ascended the stairs, her mind tumbled with escape ideas. The thought of pushing herself backward against Loverboy was foremost in her mind. One swift push would send him falling. But with the tight grip around her waist, she'd roll down with him. Her best bet lay with the handcuffs in her purse.

At the top of the stairs her legs wobbled as she poised herself to break loose when Jim jumped out to her rescue. Nothing happened.

A drop of perspiration ran down the side of her face. Another one dripped down her back.

The hallway was long. The longest hallway she'd ever walked down. She didn't know how she managed to keep herself together. Didn't know how she didn't bolt and run.

As she passed the open doorways, she heard the men's groans, the women's sensual whimpers, creaking bedsprings. The sounds didn't arouse her this time. Fear encased her body. Making her legs heavy. Making her only thought of escaping Loverboy, finding Jim, and getting the hell out of here.

When they reached her room, Sky stopped in the doorway and blinked in shock.

Candles flickered everywhere. The distinct scent of lilac filled the air. Filling her room with candles meant only one thing. He meant to have sex with her.

Chapter Seven

Terror at the prospect of being raped made her dizzy. Her insides shook. Her legs felt like jelly.

"I have to use the bathroom," she said tightly.

"I'll accompany you."

"I... I can go myself."

"No," Loverboy said firmly.

He led her into the bathroom. Her anxiety mounted when through the candlelight flickering through the open doorway, she spied her purse on the countertop. Exactly where she'd left it.

"I have protection in my purse," she said as she reached out and grabbed it.

He yanked the purse out of her hand. Sky almost screamed in frustration.

"I don't have to go anymore." She whimpered.

He grunted angrily and led her back out to the bedroom. Sky noticed the purse in his hand. It was angled in such a way she was able to ram her hand into a side pocket. A split second later, her fingers slid onto the cold metal of the handcuffs.

Loverboy's hot breath sizzled across the back of her neck, tickling the fine neck hairs. His male scent wrapped around her body, making her legs tremble with fear.

She would have to be very careful and very fast.

Sky turned around and slipped the cuff around his wrist. She was ready to snap it shut when Loverboy suddenly pushed her backward.

Flopping onto her back on the bed, Sky gasped in surprise when Loverboy grabbed both her wrists, swung her arms over her head, snapped a cuff over one wrist, slid the cuff around a wagon wheel spindle in the headboard and cuffed her other wrist, securing her to the bed.

"You son of a bitch!" Sky shouted. She tried to bring down her arms but pain ripped through her wrists.

"Please relax, Sky."

"Oh, I'll relax. When you're in a court of law brought up on kidnapping a government agent."

"Easy, honey. I already told you. I'm not going to hurt you."

"And the cuffs are just toys?" she spat.

"What else am I supposed to do when you attack me with them?"

Sky exhaled in frustration. "What are you planning to do to me?"

"Talk."

"Right!"

"About Sally Green."

"I saw Sally Green's Contract. You sold her for $300,000. You promised her $100,000. You're worse than the government. What you're doing is illegal, Loverboy."

"$100,000 a year is what I offer the slave, Sky. The rest of it is my finder's fee. I can offer you the same deal. That's more than you make in 4 years, isn't it? I can make you an expert at pleasing others and how to get someone to please you."

"I'm not for sale, Loverboy."

"No, you're not. You want to get married. Live that old fashioned dream about raising kids in a two story house with a big backyard and a white picket fence. That's where Sex Squad Detective Jim McBride comes in."

Sky bit her bottom lip as the darkest fear engulfed her. Loverboy had Jim. That's why he hadn't come to her rescue.

"Where is he?"

"He is being prepared."

"Prepared for what?"

"For your marriage, of course."

Had Loverboy gone nuts?

"I'm a preacher, Sky. You want to marry Jim. He obviously loves you. I plan to proceed over the ceremony, watch the consummation as is law and leave you two to your honeymoon."

"Why?"

"Why what?"

"Why are you forcing us to get married?"

"Forcing you? No one is forcing you, Sky. You don't have to marry him. But it might be in your best interest if you two got hitched and displayed a united front."

"What's that supposed to mean?"

"It means what Jim did to you at Sex Squad Headquarters is illegal, Sky. Sex on the job, is illegal. You were taped at Sex Squad and you were taped here while Jim gave you the trigasm. I have the tapes. If the Chief saw it you would lose both your jobs and be reprimanded."

"The Chief gave us his blessing to have sex if we needed to get your attention."

"I'm sorry, Sky, but according to the revised assignment records, you weren't supposed to have sex."

Sky swore inwardly.

The smug look on Loverboy's face meant he'd obviously fixed everything in his favor. His next words confirmed her suspicions.

"As far as Sex Squad Headquarters is concerned, Sally Green never went missing and the Chief never gave you the go ahead to engage in sexual activities. Your assignment was to merely infiltrate my farmhouse to check if I was training sex slaves illegally and get out with the information."

"You bastard! You paid someone off. Who's your contact?"

"You and Jim and the Chief are our contacts, of course. At least that's what will come out if you chose to tell anyone what transpired here." He withdrew an envelope from his back pocket. From it, he dug out a slip of paper and shoved it under her nose.

Sky's blood ran cold as she read it.

"And for all your help, here's a wire transfer, Sky. To prove you are on my payroll of course. It is for $500,000 dollars placed in your account. There's one for Jim too. You say anything to anyone and this bribe will become public knowledge."

"You can't buy my silence."

"I already have."

"You won't get away with this, Loverboy. I spoke directly to the Chief to get this assignment"

"The Chief will deny giving you permission for sexual encounters."

"Like hell he will."

"It's all been arranged, Sky. The Chief's daughter, Sally, is training in my farmhouse willingly. She wants to be a sex slave, but not for her father. If word gets out what he's been doing to her since she was eight, he'd be joining you and Jim in prison."

"You're disgusting. The Chief would never do anything to hurt his only daughter. He loves her."

"He fucks her!" Loverboy spat angrily.

"You're a liar!"

"He's telling you the truth, Sky." Jim's bitter voice curled into the room.

He stood in the door way. Naked. Anger brewed in his eyes.

"Jim! Thank God you're all right."

"Take the cuffs off her," Jim demanded as he rushed into the room.

"Keep them on, Jim. The wedding will be more exciting this way," Loverboy said.

The bed moved slightly as Jim sat down and took her into his arms.

"I'm so glad you're all right," he whispered.

"Nothing what getting out of these handcuffs won't cure."

Jim smiled as he caressed her sore shackled wrists. "Did he tell you?"

"About us getting married? Sally Green? The tapes he has on us? Or the substantial amounts of money he's stashed in our accounts?"

"I guess you know everything."

"He set us up."

Jim nodded. "A damn good job of it, too."

"Why, thank you," Loverboy cooed.

Jim threw Loverboy a cold look that made him shut up.

"Is it really true about Sally?" Sky whispered. "About the Chief abusing her since she was eight?"

"I'm afraid so. I talked to her in the Sex Dungeon. She doesn't want anything to do with her father. She's made her decision. She wants to be a sex slave. There's nothing we can do."

"Shall we get on with the ceremony and the physical consummation of the marriage?" Loverboy asked.

Jim's arms tightened around her. "Do you still want to marry me, Sky?"

His voice was filled with hope. His nearness intoxicated her and his warmth surrounded her like a cocoon, protecting her from Loverboy's prying eyes.

"With Loverboy as our preacher?"

"If it isn't him, it'll be another preacher. And I sure do want to marry you, Sky. But I'll wait until we can get another one if that's what you want."

"No."

Jim's sharp inhalation and the shocked look on his face made her realize he'd taken her the wrong way.

"I mean no, I can't wait for you. I want you inside me, Jim. I want you inside me so bad I can just scream."

He grinned. "I'll have you screaming in no time flat."

At the thought of what his hot hands would do to her body, every square inch of her skin sizzled to life.

An excited giggle escaped her lips.

Jim turned to Loverboy.

"Marry us. After you're finished we want nothing more to do with you. Do you hear me? We'll keep quiet about your goddamn Sex Slave course and Sally. But only because I want Sky protected. If it was only me in this, I'd be hanging your ass out to dry to anyone who'd listen."

Loverboy was smart enough not to say anything. The smugness zipped away from his face leaving him pale and shaken. Obviously, Loverboy realized he was lucky to get off this easily.

Jim turned back around. He smiled at her. It was a sexy smile. A teasing promise of things to come, and her heart floated wildly in her chest.

"Look into my eyes, Sky. Let's pretend it's just the two of us."

She did as he said. The look of love in his eyes burned so intensely she could swear he'd never loved her more than at this exact moment.

His brown eyes drew the breath from her lungs and she found herself drowning in his unique masculine scent. Her insides were turning to mush. The thought of what would soon be happening between them made her breasts tingle with awareness. Made moisture seep from her cunt as her body began to ready for him.

Mild air slammed against her skin as he slowly peeled her tight skirt down and off her legs. Instinctively, Sky spread her legs, allowing Jim to gaze upon her moist cunt. His eyes darkened and turned to a look of ravishing hunger.

A hunger that could only be extinguished by burying his thick rod into her aching cunt.

Excitement rippled through her like a bolt of lightning as he reached for the buttons on her blouse. Trembling fingers worked away and within seconds he pushed the flimsy material aside, fully exposing her. The mild air caressed her skin, made her nipples pucker to attention.

She heard him suck in a deep breath. Saw his eyes widen in appreciation as he gazed upon her bare breasts like he was a starving man.

She'd been invited to many weddings in her life. Watched the groom make love to the bride in front of the preacher and all their family and friends as required by law. But never had she seen such intense love in their eyes like she saw in Jim's as he gazed upon her.

When she thought of those other weddings, a tiny tinge of regret zipped through her. She'd wanted her friends to see how much she loved Jim. She'd wanted everyone to hear her screams of passion. To witness Jim sinking his massive rod into her as they consummated their marriage. Wanted them all to witness the blood stains that would show she'd been stronger than they had been because she'd saved her virginity for the man she wanted to spend the rest of her life with.

Instead, she had Loverboy as her witness. It would be a bittersweet wedding. But in the end she did have Jim. And that's all that really mattered.

"You may begin to arouse the bride-to-be," Loverboy said. His tone was now strictly professional. The lust gone from his face. He was simply a preacher presiding over their wedding.

Loverboy's words were all the encouragement Jim needed. Reaching out with both hands he cupped her heavy breasts in his hot hands, lifted them slightly as if to check their weight. It was an intimate gesture that made her breathing pick up speed.

"You're so beautiful," he whispered. "So damn beautiful."

Fire lanced through her breasts as his hands gently squeezed her softness. His thumbs arched upwards slamming over her stiff nipples.

They were highly sensitive to his touch, and Sky couldn't help but bite her lower lip to prevent from crying out. He continued this action until her breathing grew erratic and arousal soared through her body. Moments later, his index finger joined his thumb in the foray. Squeezing and plucking her nipples from their very root to their now extremely sensitized tips.

The ministrations against her breasts seemed to have unleashed an agony between her legs, too. By now her cunt was aching and drenched with need. She found herself fighting the cuffs holding her wrists hostage, pulling against them. She wanted to reach out to touch the hard rod dangling between his legs. Wanting to grab a hold of its velvet encased steel and guide its heat between her aching legs.

"Now, Jim," she begged. "Please, now."

"Not yet, Sky," he whispered gently. "I want to taste you. I want to love you."

His words were music to her ears. She wanted to wrench her arms free from the cuffs and wind them around his neck. She wanted to kiss him. To show him how much she loved him.

"I love you so much," she whispered back.

His eyes danced at her words. His fingers raked against her sensitive nipples, and she cried out as every nerve ending breathed fire.

She arched her breasts against his hands, wanting more of this fierce enjoyment.

Jim's heated rod slapped thickly against the inside of her thighs as he moved closer to her.

Sky cried out as his head lowered and his hot mouth covered a hard nipple, drawing it into his heated cavern.

He savored her. Expertly licking her plump nipples with his tongue. Nibbling their achiness with the tips of his teeth.

The sensations shimmering through her body were mind-blowing. All sane thoughts burned as they hit the flames of the nearby candles. She moaned and writhed as he licked at her with unrestrained longing.

The fire in her lower belly increased. Consumed her. She gasped at its intensity. Shuddered as Jim feasted on her breasts like a man dining on his last supper.

And then he sucked. Hard.

So hard her hips flew up off the bed and she felt the tip of his hard rod touch her clit. Lightning ripped through her cunt, making her cry out.

His mouth left her breast, leaving her nipple wet and wanting. The bed moved a little and she opened her eyes just in time to see his head lower to hers.

His mouth settled firmly over her lips, encasing her with his steely warmth. His full lips sliding against hers were a hot invitation, and she opened her mouth, welcoming him in.

His lips were tasting, loving, claiming as his moist tongue moved roughly into her mouth. Her tongue pressed against his silky one as they clashed and warred. He backed off, allowing her access to his hot, moist cavern.

He tasted dark. Delicious. And dangerous.

His kiss became restless. Fiercer. He took her mouth wildly and she met him at every turn.

Awareness zipped along her nerve fibers as the mattress dipped beneath her. He was getting ready. It was time.

Her heart thumped madly.

Sky jolted as his hot hands seared against the inside of her thighs, widening her legs even more.

Loverboy picked up the cue and cleared his throat.

"We are gathered here today to witness the joining of these two lovebirds."

Loverboy's voice faded away as Jim's hot hands slid under her butt and cupped her ass cheeks. Deep pleasure sunk into her skin where he touched. He lifted her hips and dipped his head between her legs.

His hot breath blew against her cunt, making her legs tremble. The bristle from his unshaven face seared against her sensitive skin.

Sky cried out as his hot lips kissed her swollen wet flesh. His hot tongue pushed aside her nether lips and stabbed her pleasure nub. Blistering fire ripped through her cunt.

Her breathing quickened and grew shallow as Jim's hard tongue circled her hot nub of nerves.

Circling and stabbing, then circling again.

She couldn't stop herself from whimpering as the lust rose to fever pitch.

Her body pulsed. Hummed. Begged for him to enter her.

When Jim's long hot tongue skillfully slid into her vagina, Sky's brain short circuited and her hips convulsed at the unexpected onslaught.

Sweet God above! She was spiraling out of control.

His long tongue dashed upward inside her, stopping to stroke a pleasure spot an inch or so inside her opening. Oh hell! He'd targeted her g-spot!

Her vagina muscles convulsed around his thick tongue. Before Sky knew what she was doing she'd wrapped her legs around his warm head, pulling him closer.

His tongue burrowed deeper, and she inhaled at the fantastic tension building inside her cunt. She loved the way her vaginal muscles began to contract around his hot tongue. Loved the way Jim sucked on her clit.

Lust was closing in. She could feel the pressure mount.

Her sobs ripped through the air and her cunt exploded in burning waves of pleasure. Feverish spasms wracked her body making her jerk wildly. She heard him moan erotically as she rocked her cunt against his face, her slick heat slipping into his mouth.

She sucked in ragged breaths as the pleasure spilled through her, carrying her away on the violent tremors.

When her body finally stilled, she reluctantly unclasped her legs from around Jim's head.

He withdrew his tongue and lifted his head, licking his lips greedily. His face was flushed. A cocky smile tilted his lips.

"Damn you taste good."

Sky's heart burst with love.

"Jim, I never knew it could be so... good," she whispered.

Once again his eyes grew dark with desire and the sweet agony of arousal sprang to life deep in her belly. His hot hands still cradled her ass, and Sky suddenly realized she just couldn't get enough of sex with Jim.

"More," she whispered. "Please give me more."

Her eyes fixed on Jim's massive cock. He looked so hard. He must ache terribly. Despite his discomfort, he'd taken care of her needs, instead of his.

She needed to bring him relief. Bring both of them relief. Needed to bury him inside her.

She made a grab for his cock but the handcuffs bit painfully into her wrists. The denial of reaching out to him only increased her arousal.

"You're lucky I'm tied down or I'd return the favor and send you into convulsions." She chuckled.

"Promises, promises," he whispered back.

In the background, Preacher Loverboy cleared his throat and said rather quickly, "Do you Jim McBride, take Sky O'Kelley to be your lawfully wedded wife, in sickness and in health, for richer for poorer, until death do you part?"

Jim gazed directly into Sky's eyes. The dark sexy look shining in those brown depths made her heart pound harder.

"I do," he said.

Happiness crushed Sky and hot tears slid over her warm cheeks.

"Sky O'Kelley," the preacher continued, "do you take Jim McBride to be your lawfully wedded husband? In sickness and in health, for richer, for poorer, until death do you part?

"I do," Sky whispered.

Jim smiled proudly. Pure love brewed in his eyes. Love, excitement and fiery passion.

When Jim climbed into position between her legs, Sky shivered with eagerness. His swollen tip pressed teasingly against her opening, and Sky held her breath as desire knotted her cunt.

She wished he'd just plunge into her and satisfy that deep ache. But he couldn't. Not yet. But soon.

"The ring?" Loverboy asked.

"Here." Jim awkwardly pried the ring off his little finger.

Sky couldn't help but to giggle. Where had he gotten the ring on such short notice?

"Place it on her finger."

Jim did as he was instructed. The ring fit perfectly.

"By the power invested in me, I now pronounce you husband and wife. You may consummate the marriage."

"I love you," Jim whispered and then with one violent thrust, his large swollen cock pierced her pussy.

Chapter Eight

Sky cried out as his hard steel rod caused fierce virginal pain to shoot through her insides. Jim's hot mouth fused perfectly over hers, cutting off the rest of her scream.

Thankfully, the pain faded quickly into memory and his thrust stopped.

His mouth moved over hers in a gentle sweetness she found erotic. He tasted so hot. And so good. But she wanted more. She wanted to feel his power surge inside her. She wanted to soar with the pleasure she'd experienced when he'd tongue fucked her cunt.

She couldn't help but to moan as he kissed her so hard she felt her pussy muscles contract around his shaft. He must have felt it too, for he suddenly sunk his rod deeper. His shaft was long and thick as he opened her wide, stretching the walls of her cunt.

God! He was huge. He seemed endless as he continued to push his hard shaft upward to fill her passage. Finally, she had taken all of him inside her and he stopped.

"You like?" he asked as he broke his mouth from hers.

Sky moaned in answer. She couldn't have spoken if her life depended on it. He felt so wonderful as he pulsed inside her, his glorious size filling her up.

"You're so beautiful," he whispered against her ear and to her horror he began to withdraw his hard rod.

What was he doing? Sweet heavens come back.

He drew almost all the way out and drove his throbbing flesh back inside her, hitting her most sensitive places, making her cry out in shameless abandon.

His mouth covered hers again, silencing her. His hot tongue plunged into her mouth in the same rhythm as his thrusts into her cunt. He continued this strategy, and within seconds, the frantic climax built to a feverish pitch.

He thrust harder. Fire zipped through her cunt, destroying all her sane thoughts.

Ramming her hard. She loved the feeling of being stuffed by his hardness. Loved the way her vaginal muscles sucked him in. The way his face clenched in euphoric desperation as he continued to fuck her. Loved the sounds of their hot flesh slapping against each other.

She smiled at the sound of his sexy grunts as he continued to pound into her. She arched her hips, allowing him deeper penetration. Her breath came in short spurts now as a scream began to build inside her throat.

She was teetering on the brink. One last thrust from him was all she needed.

And then it came, quickly followed by an explosion that layered over her like a canopy of fireworks. The scream flew from her mouth as her cunt shattered into sharp splinters of pleasure. Her body convulsed violently. A frantic euphoria took hold of her and carried her to the pleasure world.

His cock pumped harder and harder. Faster and faster. Violent waves of pure pleasure jolted her, making her writhe beneath her new husband.

Jim kept pumping into her like a fierce storm. She matched his every thrust.

Ecstasy snowballed inside her body, and she hung on the precipice of sweet agony and erotic pain. Peak after shocking peak of white lightning zipped through her cunt until she found another scream rip from her lungs.

Soon her powerful climax softened and sweetened into tiny shuddering convulsions.

Sky became aware of Jim's firm hands clasping her hips as he continued to thrust into her.

She watched the vulnerable look on his face as he concentrated on his thrusts. The agonizing smile on his lips. The seductive way his eyes were scrunched tightly.

A moment later, he groaned loudly. His entire body shuddered violently as his hot love liquid spilled inside her, filling her up with his heat.

Finally he went limp, collapsing on top of her. A moment later he rolled them onto their sides, leaving himself buried inside her.

Listless and satiated by her new husband's lovemaking, Sky buried her face into his warm neck.

His pulse hammered against her cheek like a lullaby making Sky smile as a wonderful peace enveloped her.

They were married.

Only minutes ago she'd thought they might have a chance at getting back together and now here she was beside the man she loved. His ring of love on her finger.

She smiled into the heat of his neck and drifted off into a hazy world of feeling loved, of getting aroused and wanting more sex.

She must have drifted off for a while for when she awoke, Jim wasn't inside her anymore. He lay beside her, cuddling her in his strong arms.

"The preacher is gone. He removed your cuffs and left the marriage license on the table." His seductive breath caressed her face. Sinfully brown eyes took her breath away.

"Everything's going to be all right now. He can't hurt us as long as we do as he says. I'll do whatever it takes to protect you and keep you from harm."

"I don't care what he threatens us with. As long as we're together we can withstand anything he throws our way."

"Spoken like a true trooper."

She found herself reacting as his heated gaze raked along her naked body. Felt the tingling tension inside her belly mounting again. Within seconds, she was so hot for him she thought she might explode.

"Now we can start the honeymoon." Jim's velvety voice made her wet between her legs.

"Fuck me, Jim. I want you to fuck me... please. I love you so much. The thought of you being outside of me for one more minute is driving me crazy."

Jim grinned and another jolt of joy rippled through her wet cunt.

Reaching out, she grabbed Jim's powerful shoulders, pulling his muscular body down on top of her.

His mouth dominated hers as he clamped tightly over her trembling lips. His hot tongue wasted no time invading her. Plunging past her teeth, he warred violently with her tongue. Sharp jabs, insistent stabs that sent a hot yearning clashing between her legs.

His scent overwhelmed her. Made her swoon. Made her wonder if maybe she'd bitten off more than she could chew.

She sensed he was a man out of control. A desperate man out for his own pleasure. And he didn't care how he got it.

His kiss continued. Hard and long until it took all breath from her lungs.

Finally, he ripped his mouth free, allowing her to gasp for air.

He anchored himself on his elbows. His chest heaved wildly and crashed against her sensitive nipples. His hard muscled thighs cradled her and his rod, thick and heavy, sat poised at the doorway of her aching vagina, waiting to enter.

He gazed down at her. His eyes were wild with desire. His full mouth bruised and swelled from the kiss.

"I've wanted you so bad for so long and now you're mine."

Heat rose in her cheeks at his comment. "I'm sorry I made you wait so long."

In answer, he nipped violently at her bottom lip. She gasped in pain. Tasted her own blood. The bite pulsed erotically.

"You bastard."

His eyes glittered with amusement at her anger.

"I could have fucked you on that desk at Sex Squad Headquarters. Slid my aching shaft into you. You were so ripe and ready. It would have been so easy."

She shivered against him at his honest words.

"But I didn't. That's when I knew I wanted you in my life forever. Knew I could wait for you. I want to father your children. I want to fuck you every morning until we are so goddamn old we can't do it anymore. That's my vow to you, Sky. Every morning I'm going to fuck you. Hard. So hard you're going to ache. So hard you're going to beg me for more. So hard you'll remember me wherever you go."

"Only every morning?" she teased.

"Anytime I want. Morning, noon and night."

"What about when I want it?"

"You'll wear me out if I listen to your wants," he growled.

Before she could blink, his lips came crushing down on hers again. Intense heat filled her mouth as his tongue plunged deep inside her. Deeper than he'd ever gone before. At the same time, his rampaging penis sliced into her cunt like a hot steel rod, releasing a pleasure so wild and so erotic, Sky had to close her eyes at its intensity.

Instinctively, she lifted her legs and dug the heels of her feet into Jim's muscular ass. The new position allowed him to penetrate deeper.

Shock and pleasure burned her cunt. His hardness was a wondrous agony. His length purely monstrous. His pulsing thickness, unbelievable.

He stopped and tore his mouth from hers again. He looked down at her. His brown eyes glowed with pride.

"You feel so good wrapped around me. I want to stay inside you forever."

"You do that and we'll never have those kids you want."

He lifted a hand and touched a long warm finger to her quivering lips.

"You've got a beautiful mouth, Sky. Lips I need to taste all the time. I can't get enough of you. You tortured me so much, denying me access to you. There were times my water bill left me penniless from all those cold showers."

"With me around, you'll be able to save money. We'll take showers and baths together."

Jim inhaled a deep breath. His rod throbbed inside her. She wanted to start gyrating her hips. Wanted him to make love to her.

"I really should punish you for making me wait so long, Sky. I should punish you real hard."

"Punish me?" Excitement slithered up her bare back.

"My penis can bring you pleasure, if I want it to. I can also use it to punish."

Sky gasped as his hot shaft suddenly pulsated inside her. Her sensitive cunt muscles contracted greedily, sending an array of pleasant sensations screaming into her womb.

His rod stopped throbbing and her muscles relaxed.

"You son of a bitch!" she gasped. Her cunt ached for more.

"Did you like that?"

"Give me your best shot, Jim." she breathed, wanting him to do it again.

The corners of his lips curled upwards. "You don't scare easy do you?"

"I don't have time to be scared, not with your massive punishing tool pulsing inside me. Go ahead, let's see what you're made of."

He nipped on her bottom lip again. Ran his tongue along the tender bite he'd inflicted with his sharp teeth only moments earlier.

It hurt. She shivered.

His head curled into the curve of her neck. He kissed her there, a feather light kiss and then he nipped her hard.

Pain sizzled through her neck.

She tried to squirm away from him. She couldn't.

His iron rod impaled her cunt. Held her nicely in place.

"Son of a bitch," She whispered again.

He grinned and whispered, "A birthday hickie for the birthday gal. Happy Birthday, Sky."

He shifted the upper part of his body until his chest rested lightly against her nipples. And then his hands were there. Covering both her breasts.

His palms were kneading, grabbing, hurting.

Sky shot him a look of surprise at his roughness. His eyes twinkled with enjoyment.

His kissed her cheeks with hot silky caresses. A direct contrast to the way his hands groped her breasts and tweaked her nipples painfully.

"You call this punishment?" She hissed between her teeth.

He rolled his hips and his rod grew harder inside her cunt. Her vaginal muscles quivered with delight, tried to convulse and failed because he'd stopped again.

His mouth moved to her ear and he purred. "I call that punishment."

"Damn you!" She wanted him to fuck her. Not torture her.

He pulled at her nipples and he caught her gasp with his warm mouth.

Her breasts felt as if they were on fire beneath the ministrations of his possessive palms. Her nipples were hard nubs and sharply sensitive.

Her head began to swirl. Her limbs weakened. Strange sensations began to unfurl along the nerve endings in her breasts. In her cunt. In her lips and mouth. The vibrations grew, spreading wildly.

They were intoxicating. She found herself whimpering at the flames grabbing hold of her body.

Soon her entire body writhed beneath him on its own volition.

"That's it, don't fight it."

"What the hell are you doing to me?" She gasped.

God! This felt fantastic.

His hands drew away from her breasts and his chest came down on top of her nipples, flattening her sensitive breasts against his hard chest.

And then she felt his hand slip between her legs, to her wet pleasure bud.

She jolted when he touched her firmly. She thought she just might burst into an inferno or die of internal combustion.

His finger began rubbing her bud. Hard. His roughness made her pant. Made her moan.

She could feel her body begin to tense with want. With the need for fulfillment.

God, she hoped he wouldn't stop! She couldn't take it if he did.

"Please," she whimpered.

"Please, what?"

"Fuck me. Now. Dammit!"

He didn't say anything. His hand stilled.

Sky moaned.

No! Not again. Don't stop!

He didn't move a muscle.

Sky opened her eyes in time to see the heated expression in his eyes. The trembling pulse in his neck as he restrained himself from withdrawing and plunging into her again and again, giving them both the satisfaction they craved.

"Please...."

"You think you've been punished enough?"

"Yes… Oh my Gosh! I can't take it anymore."

It was all he needed to hear.

His silk cased iron rod ripped out of her, and he plunged right back through her slit again. Hitting her most sensitive spots on the way in, making Sky cry out.

His finger rubbed fiercely.

Her pleasure bud ached. Hurt. And he kept rubbing. And thrusting into her like a piston.

Filling her. Fucking her.

Her body convulsed around him. Sweet pain and pure pleasure ripped her apart. Waves of it. It kept coming and coming.

Washing over her like a tidal wave of lust.

Sky squeezed her eyes tighter and she arched wildly beneath Jim's massive onslaught.

The scent of their lovemaking filled her nostrils, turned her on even hotter.

An orgasm shuddered through her body. And then another. Quickly followed by a stream of them.

His erection surged inside her and she screamed out when the flames engulfed her body and his hot love seed shot deep inside her....

* * * *

Sky awoke to sunshine streaming through her windows and to an interesting tapping sound coming from somewhere in the house.

At first she didn't know where she was and then reality crashed over her in one wonderful breath sucking wave.

Last night, Jim had married her!

And he'd made love to her at the same time. And she hadn't been in the least bit embarrassed about her nudity. Unbelievable.

Sky stretched her aching legs and winced at the soreness in her cunt.

Oh God!

Jim had been so big when he'd fucked her good and hard. And she'd loved it.

She lifted her left arm from under the sheets and looked at her ring finger. A gold ring glittered up at her.

She couldn't help but smile. She was married to a man she loved with all her heart. A man who vowed to fuck her every morning.

And it was morning....

So? Where was he?

"Jim!" she called out.

No answer.

The farmhouse seemed quiet. Deserted? Except for that strange tapping sound coming from somewhere.

Sky climbed out of bed and searched for her clothes. They were gone again.

Perhaps Jim was playing games and wanted her to go looking for him. She could do that. And when she found him....

Wrapping the sheet around her, she winced at the tenderness in her cunt. Tiptoeing to the open doorway, she peeked out into the hallway.

Silence. Where was her hubby? Where were all the students and Loverboy and Carmella?

She walked down the hallway and looked in the bedrooms as she passed. All the beds were neatly made. All the rooms were empty.

The only sign that anyone had been here were the dozens of unlit candles placed throughout each room.

Downstairs, she found a red envelope taped to the inside of the front door.

Dear Sky,

Please find enclosed copies of the wire transfers of the $500,000 into your bank account and another $500,000 dollars into Jim's personal bank account. Now that you are married you both are millionaires. It is up to you if you consider this money as a wedding gift or a bribe.

On the VCR in the living room you will find three CD's.

One CD is of your trigasm escapade with Jim. One CD of your wedding. One CD showing Jim finger fucking you at Sex Squad Headquarters. These are not the only copies. After viewing them, I trust you will remain silent about the Sex Slave Courses.

If you choose not to remain silent, you will not have the Chief's blessing. It has already been added to your records that you were instructed not to engage in any sexual activity during this assignment. Tsk. Tsk. Tsk. With those three tapes and the bribe, that's four Sex Strikes against you.

Should you break your silence, the CDs and the bank receipt will be released to the Sex Squad High Commission. Rest assured they will ensure your silence. Compliments of me.

Sky's stomach dropped as if she were on an elevator. She'd believed in the Three Sex Strikes and Life policy. Anyone breaking the Sex rules, one of which was no sex during work hours, had only three chances. When they had three strikes it was off to Sex State Prison for life. Life without sex.

God help them both. Jim and she had four strikes.

She'd voted for the Three Sex Strikes and Life Policy herself. Never in her wildest dreams did she think she'd end up having the law used against her in such a way.

Sky bit her bottom lip. Sweet Jesus.

Could she trust Loverboy to not release those tapes? It would be in his best interest not to. If he did release them, he'd be dragged into the foray. And attention was the last thing Loverboy was looking for. Especially since he was training Sex Slaves without the government's permission.

Sky nodded her head at that last thought. Yes, Loverboy would keep quiet. And so would they. No need to get too upset with all this trouble hanging over their heads like a guillotine.

If they didn't keep quiet, they would be locked away in tiny cages in the Sex State Prison and there would be no sex for life.

Unbidden came a vision of Jim. Of how he had made her scream last night. She could still remember the rough feel of his callused thumb as he'd frantically kneaded her passion bud.

Remembered the way the round, smooth tip of his massive cock had thrust in and out of her aching cunt without mercy. He had just about drove her crazy as her body had been ripped apart by climax after climax. She didn't think she could have had so many, and he'd just kept hammering into her until they all had clashed into one violent explosion.

Obviously, Jim knew how to love a woman. And he'd shown her so much more of what he was made of on their honeymoon.

She glanced out the door's small window. No cars or trucks in the driveway. Loverboy and everyone else had fled.

No use wearing her toga sheet anymore. She dropped the sheet onto the floor and headed into the living room.

The CD's were set on top of the CD player. All were clearly marked.

Sky looked at them and sighed. They'd have to keep these tapes safe. Away from prying eyes. And she'd have to trust Loverboy to keep his copies safe, too.

Dammit! It wasn't the greatest feeling knowing you were set up by Loverboy. But they would survive. And they would love each other every day.

That insistent rapping sound started up again. Sky tilted her head and listened to the slow tap tap coming out of the heating vent.

Seemed as if some sort of pattern was arising.

Morse Code?

Someone sending her a message?

In the basement. Help.

Oh my God!

In the basement? Where was the basement?

She scanned the living room. Aside from Loverboy's office door, she saw no other doors.

Heart pounding against her naked chest, Sky raced into the kitchen and skidded to a halt.

One section of the wall was pushed aside, revealing a secret door.

Turning the knob, Sky opened the door to discover a steep staircase disappearing into a dimly lit hall. The tapping continued with the same insistent message.

It had to be from Jim. They'd done something to him. They'd hurt him some way.

Gasping frantically, Sky couldn't run down the stairs fast enough. When she reached the bottom, she felt overwhelmed at all the doors. Gathering her senses, she counted three doors on each side of the hallway. The last one to the right was open.

Racing down the hallway, Sky peered in. And froze at the sight.

Chapter Nine

Sky's new hubby lay on a table. Legs and arms spread eagle and strapped down. He had a ball gag in his mouth which prevented him from speaking.

Desire soaked his brown eyes when he saw her enter.

"They had to tie you down to keep you from running out on me?"

A chuckle escaped around the ball gag.

His eyes watched her every move as she approached the table he lay upon. Circling the table, she examined every inch of his naked body. She was overwhelmed as her gaze raked over the sleek muscles of his chest, over his flat stomach.

When her eyes latched onto Jim's thick, vein riddled penis, Sky couldn't stop her intense need to touch him.

He moaned the instant her fingers curled around his silk encased steel rod. His powerful erection burned a promise into her skin. Burned and pulsed and grew like a writhing snake. Grew into a taut, rigid cock. A cock she wanted to taste so bad, her mouth watered.

"Looks like we're free to carry on with our honeymoon. Loverboy and his friends have flown the coop," Sky said as she slid the tips of her fingers up one side of his rigid shaft, over his head and then down the other side.

He wiggled beneath her touch. His cute lips tightened over the ball gag.

"You like that do you?"

He tried to move his head in answer, but the restraints prevented him from fully cooperating with an answer.

"Is that shake of your head a yes? Or a no?" Sky ran her finger back up over his bulging tip. He shuddered beneath her touch.

"I'll have to believe you've nodded a yes."

She bent over until she was face to face with his rigid member. It's one eyed slit stared up at her. He was pulsing and thick, and Sky remembered how it had throbbed inside her last night. Now it was her turn to give back to her husband a little of what she'd experienced while handcuffed to the bed, and then later when he'd taken her so hard, she'd almost screamed for his mercy.

She licked her lips in anticipation.

In one open mouthed thrust, she slid her lips over the entire puffed head of his rod. He groaned loudly at the assault.

He was hot in her mouth. Hot and pulsating and oh so deliciously hard. His hips bucked upward, shoving him deeper into her mouth.

She smiled inwardly. The way his hips thrust his penis into her mouth, he needed some release.

Real bad.

Sky pursed her lips and began to suck, ever so gently.

He moaned. A tight sound escaped the ball gag in his mouth.

She sucked harder. Jim's hips convulsed violently, and she tasted the sweetness of his pre-come in her mouth.

She liked the taste of him. Liked the taste of man. She sucked harder and flicked her tongue down along his stiff shaft.

Jim's penis tensed. He was ready to come.

Sky stopped her ministrations and lifted her head from her feast. A groan of protest growled low in his throat.

She looked into his anguished face, into his dark brown eyes. A hot core of desire brewed there, and she felt her cunt moisten with need.

Wondering how long she could stall him before he became angry enough to give her a good fucking, she smiled down at him with satisfaction. A little torture was good for a man and his penis.

"How did you make that tapping sound anyway?" She asked, swiftly changing the subject.

A furious mumble escaped from around the ball gag.

"Oh yes, I better remove this fun thing. We'll save it for later."

She leaned over and unhooked the ball gag. He pushed it away with his tongue.

"Just fuck me, will you?" he gasped.

"Not so fast, sweet hubby. Answer my question. How'd you get my attention? Better yet, how did you know I was upstairs?"

"Carmella and Loverboy set me up down here. For you. At my request."

Sky's breath hitched in her throat. "For me?"

"You can do what ever you want to me."

"I kind of get that picture. But why?"

"Because I want you happy. I want you to experience sex in every way. Besides it wasn't fair for you to have been handcuffed to the bed last night."

"I didn't mind at all once the action started."

"You are so beautiful, Sky."

"Cut to the chase, darling. Why this table?"

"It's called the passion rack. I thought maybe we could try this table out? Take turns?"

Holy. The man was going to kill her with all this exciting new stuff. This could develop into one very interesting marriage.

"In answer to your first question. When Loverboy and Carmella strapped me to the table, they told me I'd have to figure out a way on my own to get your attention. By the time I heard you walking around upstairs I'd figured out this ingenious way...." Jim arched his hips upward and then crashed his ass down onto the table with enough force to make the table wiggle, allowing it to give off a loud tap.

She didn't miss the wince on his face when his butt hit the board.

"Lift you ass again," she instructed.

He did as she instructed. Sky bent over and noticed the tiny tacks lining the board. Tiny enough so they would cause pain but not big enough to draw blood.

His ass cheeks were red with tiny indentations.

"You're going to need some TLC on those cheeks, honey."

She didn't miss the corners of his lips curve upwards into an eager smile.

"Not quite yet. First we're going to give this table a workout."

She examined the tacks and nodded in understanding. "Pain makes the brain secrete endorphins. Endorphins counteract pain and creates pleasure. Very ingenious."

Could she achieve extreme pleasure with Jim, through pain? Something to ponder on their honeymoon.

"Can you at least suck me off and give me some relief before you get started?"

"Ummmm, nope."

Jim inhaled a sharp breath as she wrapped both hands around his thick pleasure stick, relishing the powerful heat he gave off.

"I still want to taste other parts of you. It might take me some time."

The excruciating look on Jim's face made Sky smile. She had the power over him. She could do whatever she wanted to him. Get whatever she wanted. All with his blessing.

This was a nice feeling.

"Did Loverboy say when he was coming back?" Sky asked.

She saw the look of hesitation in his eyes.

"Tell the truth." She coaxed.

"Two weeks. Long enough for a proper honeymoon. His gift to us."

"Good. Very good. This will give us time to acquaint ourselves with each other, shouldn't it?"

Jim nodded, the smile back on his face again. Obviously he was looking forward to getting fucked morning noon and night.

Maybe she should teach him to be careful of what he wished for....

* * * *

Sky stepped out of his field of vision. Footsteps plodded quietly to the base of the table he lay on. He watched as Sky moved in between his spread-eagle legs.

When her soft, warm hands cupped his ass, he sucked in a sharp breath.

What the hell was she up to?

"Relax, my love."

His heart galloped as her fingers began to massage his ass with soothing little circles. Within seconds his ass cheeks began to tingle, and she casually moved inwards.

There was no mistaking where she was headed. Toward the crack in his ass.

Soon, her delicate fingers arrived at their destination and Jim waited anxiously to see what would happen next.

With feather light strokes, she traced the entire length of both sides of his crack, ending just beneath his hardening balls.

She retreated. He exhaled a shuddering breath.

Then she slid back again.

Back and forth, until the outer edges of his crack were on fire with arousal.

He found himself groaning in protest when she stopped.

A moment later, her face pressed intimately against his ass cheeks. The suddenness of it, hell the shock of it, sent his hips soaring upwards involuntarily and then down onto the board and the tacks he lay on. Sparkles of pain ripped through his ass cheeks, making him gasp.

"Pain heightens the pleasure centers," she said. He didn't miss the laughter in her voice.

Something warm and moist pressed against the outside edges of his asshole.

Her tongue!

Damned if a woman had ever gone near his ass with her tongue before. It felt strange and oddly exciting.

Jim sucked in another breath as her hands pulled his ass cheeks wider apart. Wider and yet wider.

Then her tongue began a slow circle like a vulture hovering over its prey. She began licking the outer edges of his hole. Teasing it with little stabs.

Extraordinary growls drifted to his ears and Jim realized with shock the foreign sound was coming from him!

His breathing became labored. Shallow.

Damned if he wasn't enjoying these interesting new sensations shimmering along his skin toward his balls.

He bucked violently when Sky's hot tongue unexpectedly stabbed into his hole. Nerves he never knew existed flickered to life as her long, moist tongue burrowed inward at an agonizingly slow pace.

He groaned when she stopped. He could feel her deep inside his anal canal. Could feel his muscles grip tightly around her tongue, as she thickened it and relaxed it. The alluring intrusion made his ass pulse with fire.

Her nose stabbed into the area between his balls, creating a fantastic pressure in his hot penis and scrotum area.

His cock swelled until it ached.

Slowly, she slithered her way out.

Jim shuddered as she drove in again. This time his ass muscles contracted quickly around her tongue sucking her deeper inside him. She withdrew again, leaving Jim waiting and wanting more.

Jesus. If someone had told him he'd be getting tongue fucked up his butt, he would have said there was no such thing. And here he was responding like a damn pro.

He wondered where on earth Sky had ever thought about tongue fucking him? Perhaps this is what she meant by wanting to taste parts of him. Holy, looked like they were going to experience quite the marriage.

Something cold and hard pressed up against his hole, making Jim stiffen in alarm.

"Shh. Relax. Trust me. I'm going to insert a butt plug."

A butt plug!

"It's been nicely lubricated and shall go in easily enough now that I've programmed your muscles to receive it."

God, she sounded like a pro already.

"It will increase your pleasure later on," she whispered.

Later on? At her words, Jim forced himself to relax his muscles as the foreign object slipped into his hole and began a slow crawl inward. To his astonishment, his hips began to shake and undulate of their own volition. The result, sharp jabs of pain in his ass cheeks from the tacks on the board.

The butt plug began to feel uncomfortable. And yet it kept filling him like he'd never been filled before.

A tinge of panic swept over him. How long was this thing? Was it ever going to end?

He almost shouted at her to stop, but a strange feeling zipped along his anal nerves. It was a nice sensation. He liked it a lot.

Suddenly his anal ring swallowed the butt plug. His ass felt full and quivered erotically.

Jim exhaled shakily.

Footsteps echoed through the silence, and Sky reappeared into his field of vision. She smiled down at him. He felt his heart tighten with love.

"That wasn't too bad, was it?" she said, echoing his earlier thought. "How does it feel?"

"Like something is in my ass," He joked.

"You'll be glad it's in for what I have planned for you."

"And exactly what is that?" He tried to keep the excitement in check.

She said nothing and moved out of his field of vision again.

He heard movement somewhere in the far corner of the room but couldn't see her. Then she began to hum.

"Sky? What are you up to?"

"Just give me a minute. I've got a surprise for you."

The sweet sexy sound of her voice made his heart begin to thump loudly in his ears. He got the feeling he was going to like what she was planning for him.

A minute later, something slid across the floor toward his right side.

A warm arm sliced across his waist and he watched in stunned fascination as Sky hoisted herself up. Her large breasts swayed as she stood and placed her legs wide apart, touching the outside of his shoulders. It gave him a damned fascinating view of her pussy.

And a freshly shaved pussy at that.

"You like the new look?" she purred as she gazed down at him.

"Holy shit," he breathed.

He couldn't help but to respond at this visual sight.

His balls tightened even more, if that were possible. His shaft felt so rigid he was sure he'd come any second.

He'd read somewhere that guy's brains were wired differently than women's. Women became sexually aroused when they were cuddled and told warm, fuzzy things, like he'd been doing with Sky over the past weeks. Men, on the other hand were aroused by something visual. And looking straight up into Sky's freshly shaven warm and waiting cunt was definitely visual.

And sexually stimulating.

Her clit looked purple and swollen from arousal. He couldn't help but notice the thin stream of juice running down the insides of her thighs.

Obviously tonguing his ass had turned her on. Go figure. He was learning something new every few minutes about his new bride.

"Pleasure me, slave," she demanded, and she began to squat.

His mouth watered as her cunt lowered into just the right position over his face. Using his tongue, he pried apart her swollen nether lips, zeroing upward onto her passion bud.

She gasped and bucked violently as he circled her hard clit area with slow torturous jabs. She was already very much aroused at this new sexual position.

Since she'd had a little bit of fun torturing him when she'd latched onto his penis with her mouth only moments earlier and hadn't given him relief, perhaps he should return the favor....

"You taste so damn good, Sky," he whispered to her.

"Tongue fuck me, Jim," her voice sounded tortured. Raw. Sensual. Beautiful.

He closed his eyes and probed around her sweet heat, taking his time as he circled her velvety pleasure bud in torturous circles.

She was coming now. Real hard. Her hips were quivering and she pressed her cunt into his face as if it were fruit going through a juice squeezer. Up and down. Side by side.

He kept his tongue speared straight up as she used it as her pleasure rod.

His own hips where gyrating as he imagined his thick shaft replacing his tongue as he speared into her warm welcoming cavern. The butt plug created some fantastic sensations of their own, sparking a cascade of spasms through his ass as his hips crashed up and down on the painful tacks.

Fresh whiffs of her sex made him headier, made his body harden with need. Christ! The woman was killing him by denying his rod access to her cunt and he would pay her back big time.

A high pitched wail broke from her throat and ripped through the air. Arching her hips into his face, she climaxed, marking him with her sexy scent.

When she came down from her high, she lifted herself from his face and on trembling legs, she stood once again, giving him a perfect view of her juicy swollen cunt.

Jim shivered with frustration. His rod was hard enough it could drill holes. He was good and ready to replace his tongue with his penis.

His breath came in shallow spurts. His heart pounded in his ears. And he anxiously waited to see what Sky was going to do next.

"You are an exquisite lover, my slave," she praised. "And now you shall be rewarded."

When her velvety hand wrapped firmly around the base of his raw pulsing shaft, his erection shuddered violently. Her moist warm mouth welcomed him, and Jim groaned as her lips firmly encased his hard flesh.

"Oh God!" He managed to groan as her sweet tongue slid erotically against the underneath part of his rod, stoking the fire into a molten lava.

His scrotum grew tight with pain. His shaft hardened with excruciating need.

And when she sucked....

His whole body just blew apart.

His hips began to thrust upward into her moist mouth. Her tongue curled erotically around his pulsing shaft and his ass fell back onto the passion rack. The tacks rammed into his sensitive skin, causing mild pain to seared his ass cheeks. The butt plug slammed deeper into his ass, causing him to gasp at the sparkling sensations ripping through him.

Holy shit! The woman sure knew how to torture him.

His body was tight with need. The pressure in his loins was fantastic.

She continued to suck him. Her warm lips sealing his shaft as if he were her prisoner.

Her hands tightened around his base, her other hand flew to his scrotum area, kneading his balls until he could stand it no longer.

"Sky!" he managed to gasp in warning.

Suckling sounds rent the air as she continued the blow job.

He couldn't wait. Couldn't hold onto these aching wonderful sensations any longer. The need for release was too overpowering.

Jim cut loose and spewed his load deep into her throat, surprised to discover she only sucked harder, firmer, as she tried to drain all of his seed from his body....

* * * *

Sky couldn't help but smile at Jim's relaxed features as he lay on the passion table, his chest heaving from the blow she'd just given him.

"Jesus, Sky," he whispered. "You're becoming a goddamn pro at this."

"I'll take that as a compliment."

"You've damn near wiped me out."

Disappointment shot through her. "Are you saying you're ready to call it quits? Have a bowl of wheaties and pick up later?"

"No way. We trade places," Jim cooed. "And I'm going to give you the fucking of your life."

"You are, are you? I like the sound of that." She laughed and eagerly untied his restraints.

"I want to hear the sound of your screams when I make you come, Sky. It's a good thing we're out here in the middle of nowhere, because I'm going to make you come so many times, the windows are going to shatter."

"Keep talking that way, big guy and I'll be coming before you even start."

"Come here," he whispered.

He curled his now free arms around her waist, guiding her down on top of his naked body. Sweet hunger gripped her insides as she felt his hard contours snuggle against her soft curves. She loved the feel of his male skin against hers. Loved the aching throbbing deep inside her cunt at the feel of his rapidly reviving bulge pushed intimately between her legs.

"Have I told you how much I love you this morning?" he whispered. His eyes darkened as he awaited her answer.

"I don't think so."

"I love you, Sky. Every minute that goes by I feel it growing."

Sky couldn't help but laugh.

His eyes darkened in surprise. "I tell my woman I love her and she laughs. What's so funny?"

"You're growing all right," she muttered as she slowly slid her hands down the sides of his hard lean waist, loving the feel of the male planes against her fingertips as she slowly headed for his hot blossoming shaft.

"I hate to break this mood," she whispered as she gently bit his lower lip. "But what are we going to do about Loverboy? And all this stuff he has hanging over our heads?"

"We wait."

"That's what I figured we should do too."

His hands slid from her waist to cup the back of her neck.

"That doesn't mean we'll do anything he wants us to do. You have to remember he won't release those CDs. Not unless he wants to incriminate himself. So we're safe as long as we keep our mouths shut."

"I can do that." Sky nibbled his upper lip. His hard body shivered with excitement below her.

"Rest assured I won't stop trying to find a way to get his copies of us together," he said softly. "It's just going to take some time. Maybe years. In the meantime, don't touch any of the money he placed in our accounts. It's evidence."

"You're reading my mind," she said and curled her lips against the warmth of his neck. The pounding of his pulse quickened as her hands slid around his thickening erection. She loved the velvety feel of his skin. The wonderful power running through his rod.

"Uh uh uh. Not yet. Are you reading my mind?" He groaned against her ear.

"My turn on the rack?"

"Damn straight," he said softly.

He clamped his mouth over hers. The heat of his lips sliding over hers was dangerously heavy with the promises of things to come, making her ache erotically in all the right places.

This was going to be one hell of a honeymoon, she thought to herself.

And it was.

The End

A HITMAN FOR HANNAH

PROLOGUE

Many years into the future....
Earth--The States
Six weeks earlier....

"You always have such a wonderfully tight ass, my Hannah."

Hannah inhaled sharply as the hard tip of Simon's lubricated shaft stretched her ass muscles.

"Just like your mother. God bless her soul. Smooth as satin. The sweetest, tightest ass." He heaved his hips against her, and his rod sunk deeper.

Warmth draped against her back as his hot hands reached around her to tenderly clasp on the nipple clamps he insisted she wear on the nights he bedded her.

The clamps pinched a little, but when he switched on the vibrator, her nipples responded erotically and tightened into hard aching beads of need.

With his cock buried inside her, he slowly bent her upper body forward over the padded bar stool, allowing her breasts to dangle hungrily for his touch.

"I've got a surprise for you, my darling Hannah," he whispered, "Tonight will be our last night together."

She couldn't help but breathe a little sigh of relief. She was getting bored wearing vibrating nipple clamps, walking around with butt plugs and putting up with his anal fetish.

Her joy however was short lived.

"In a couple of months you'll be twenty-one years old. I know you were eligible for the Breeding Slave status when you reached twenty, and I admit I've been selfish by keeping you all to myself, but something special happened today. A very influential and rich young couple engaged to be married dropped by the Plantation. They were looking for the parents for their first child. They saw you, Hannah, and they made me an offer I could not refuse."

Hannah tried hard not to tense up at his words, but he must have noticed her reaction because his next words were calm and somewhat soothing.

"Shhh, darling. I know this is unexpected. I know you have the right to keep your first born, and you will. The couple is willing to wait for your second child. So, it's best we get started right away so that you'll be ready to go at it again right after your first-born is here. That's why I've decided that tomorrow will be the first day of your Breeding Ceremony."

"How wonderful!" She forced her voice to remain lively and upbeat the way her mother had taught her.

Inside though, her guts churned anxiously at the thought of being secured like a trapped farm cow in the Breeding barn for weeks on end, if not for months. Her body bent at the waist over a cushioned bar, much as she was now, her cunt and anus exposed so the men could line up to fuck her whenever they wanted until she got pregnant.

"I've picked out the Ceremonial gown. Of course it's the traditional red coloring, but it's made of the finest, softest see through silk. And since this will be your first child and there is no preference for who the father should be, I've decided that all my sons will have equal opportunity to bed you. They were all very pleased to hear the news, especially Jacob."

At the mention of Jacob Romero, Hannah's heart picked up speed.

"I sent him a message letting him know about your Ceremony."

"He's coming home?"

"He's coming home."

Hannah inhaled softly.

Sweet God! For years she'd longed to see the eldest Romero brother again. To look upon his handsome face. To finally have his powerful muscles beneath her fingertips as she clenched his broad back. To feel his hard thighs cradle her hips as he plunged into her. But most of all she ached to find out if the rumors about his lovemaking were true.

The thought of seeing him again after four long years made her insides ignite with a want so compelling she almost cried out at its intensity.

"I look forward to seeing him," she whispered, trying hard not to let Simon see how excited she was getting at the thought of Jacob coming home.

"You're such a sweet young woman. Just like your mother

was."

The urge to tell him she was not as stupid as her mother was so great she almost said it out loud, but his hard cock was sliding back out of her ass, and she forced herself to relax.

Past experience had taught her that Simon loved to fuck hard and fast. If she kept herself relaxed and he finished quickly, it would leave her plenty of time to put her plan into motion.

"I'm sure my boys will go easy on you."

"The more the merrier." She tried to forget the fact it was expected she be shared with all the brothers including Jacob. But from the first time she'd met the eldest Romero brother she'd known instinctively he was the only man for her.

"I know six men is a handful for your first Ceremony, but from the stories I've heard, your mother took five brothers in her first Ceremonial until she was pregnant with you. Every day she was begging them to sink their dicks into her juicy cunt, just like you'll be begging for my boys."

She inhaled sharply as his hot fingers spread her labia lips in order to stroke her clit.

"You and the Romero brothers will produce such a beautiful child, I have no doubt. Your midnight black hair and my boy's sharp blue eyes will make a fantastic combination. And, of course, as tradition dictates, your first-born will be yours to keep until he or she is sixteen. I only hope she will be a girl as sweet and as tight as you."

For the first time in a long time, Hannah found herself smiling.

But it was a bittersweet smile.

She would never allow Simon to have any of her children. And she would never have the opportunity of finding out if those rumors about Jacob were true.

Because tonight she was leaving. Tonight she was running.

Chapter One

Six weeks later....

Her cunt was tight. Damn tight. And damned hot as Jacob Romero slid in and out of her in an achingly sensual rhythm. Beneath him, Hannah moaned erotically, her body shuddered wildly as she enjoyed what he was doing to her.

He knew she'd be like this. Knew she'd be the one woman for him.

He thrust harder into her. Deeper. Her cries of passion rang like music in his ears.

The pressure inside his penis mounted. He was going to come soon. The moist heat of her cunt muscles spasmed around his thick flesh, welcoming him in, sending shards of lightning zipping up his shaft straight into his belly.

Oh yes! He was going to come.

Clenching his jaws together, his body shuddered, and he released his hot load deep into her very core....

The screeching sound of a seagull's cry ripped Jacob Romero from his erotic fantasy.

He blinked wildly at the softness of the ocean wind caressing his face. Listened to the waves as they roared onto the sand rippled beach. For a moment he was lost in this natural beauty. The reason for being here totally forgotten.

He shielded his eyes from the blazing sun as it dipped quickly to the horizon, casting a golden hue over the sexy black haired woman.

Hannah Roberts.

Breeder Slave.

Runner.

She stood on the beach. Not more than twenty feet away from him.

It was a crime she looked so good in clothes. A bigger crime that he'd been the one sent to kill her.

Jacob gritted his teeth in sudden anger. He'd never thought about not doing what he'd been trained to do. But now as he looked at his sweet innocent Hannah, he couldn't stop the aching weariness sweeping over him. A weariness that made him realize he was sick and tired of killing people.

He wanted out of this nightmare job.

Unfortunately, there was no way out. He was the eldest son, and it was proclaimed the eldest member of any free family would dedicate their lives to being a Hitman or Hitgal. He hadn't been given a choice. Hadn't been able to follow his own yearnings in life.

And one of those yearnings had been taking Hannah for his very own.

His gaze drew back to her. To her long black hair flying in the salty breeze.

Her tank top hugged generous breasts. White shorts revealed wide hips and long legs. Ocean waves lapped at her sexy bare feet.

He wondered what her toes would taste like. Marveled at how smooth those legs would feel against his lips as he planted tiny kisses along her flesh until he'd finally nestle between her legs to suckle her sweet clit.

Her laughter broke into his thoughts.

She watched a white seagull soar over her head. Her laughter was unbelievably beautiful. More beautiful than he remembered. It crashed into his ears and cracked the iciness lining his heart.

For a split second he almost turned around. Almost left her there. Almost let her go.

But he couldn't do it. He couldn't let her get away.

Slowly he lifted the rifle.

Inhaling a deep shuddering breath, he pressed the butt of the weapon hard against the crook of his shoulder. He took a bead on Hannah, and his trembling finger tightened on the trigger....

* * * *

Hannah Roberts couldn't stop laughing. She was absolutely delirious with happiness. Within the hour she'd be picked up by a boat and whisked away north of the border. To the Free States.

Sweet heavens, the impatience of waiting was driving her crazy.

Hugging the cell phone to her breasts, she remembered the whispery voice of the man who'd called last night and told her to come to the beach. He'd sounded kind and gentle and extremely mysterious. Nonetheless, at this point in time she was desperate. She was almost out of food and quite anxious to get a new start in life.

She couldn't wait to inhale freedom's fresh air. Couldn't wait to start living on her own terms.

Nobody would ever tell her what to do again. No man would be allowed to screw her any time he wished. And most of all, the fear of having to go through her first Breeding Ceremony would finally fade away.

Another fierce gust whipped against her body making her stumble backward. Making her smile into the hot sunshine as the warm sand grains sifted through her naked toes.

Six weeks ago she would never have thought she'd be standing here. Standing on an ocean beach in Northern Oregon waiting to rendezvous with the Underground Railroad who smuggled runaway Breeder Slaves to the Free States.

Six weeks ago her owner, Simon, was doing whatever he wanted to do to her. His lecherous hands fondling her aroused cunt as he pushed himself into her tight ass.

Thank God those days were gone.

She'd escaped. Taken the bundle of food she'd stashed in the attic of his home and stolen the abandoned relic of a car from one of her master's many secluded barns. Thanks to her job as a tractor driver in the Plantation fields she knew how to drive. It had made the escape much easier.

Over the years, she'd listened to the other Breeder Slaves as they'd whispered about the Underground Railway. Listened to where she should go when the time was right to leave. In her mind she'd mapped out an escape route, and it had led her here.

The rusty windmill on the hill with the sharp blue ocean backdrop had made her heart quicken with relief. Nestled in the tree-enshrouded grove she'd spied the deserted stone mansion with the faded aqua colored shutters and the lone octagonal window in the attic.

The area had looked exactly as The Breeder Slaves had said. And they'd also insisted if a runner stayed in the mansion long enough someone would come for them and whisk them off to freedom.

Hannah had stayed there almost two weeks.

Doubt had plagued her during the stay. Perhaps it had just been rumors? Perhaps no one would come for her?

But yesterday, she'd been out exploring along the beach, and when she'd come back she'd found the cell phone on the back veranda in plain sight. And beneath the phone a white note had fluttered in the breeze.

Don't be afraid. It had said. I will call tonight.

And the cell phone had rang, the mysterious voice giving her instructions to meet on the beach.

Now she was here. Standing at the arranged rendezvous point waiting to be taken away to freedom.

"Hannah." The sound of his familiar voice ripped through her like a sharp knife. For a minute, Hannah could do nothing but stand frozen as her brain tried to decipher the fact that she'd been caught.

Caught by Jacob. The only man she'd ever wanted.

Jacob. A Hitman who was here to bring her back to his father's Breeder Plantation.

Her newfound peace crashed in around her.

"Sweet mercy! No!" she heard herself whisper.

"Do as I say, and everything will be fine," he said.

Her heart crashed against her chest. She clamped down on the hysteria threatening to engulf her.

"Turn around. Nice and slow," he instructed.

Hannah didn't know if she could do it. Dizziness swirled, making her unsteady. The cell phone dropped from her hand.

She didn't know how, but she managed to turn around and came face to face with Jacob.

Her breath seized up in her lungs at the sight of him. Oh God! She'd missed him so much it hurt just to look at him.

He was taller than she remembered. Wider in the shoulders. His shoulder length hair was stringy and dirty brown. Dark stubble etched his chin, his upper lips, the sides of his full mouth.

The familiar sparkle he'd always toted for her when he'd looked at her in the past was gone, replaced by the deadest darkest blue eyes she'd ever seen.

And he pointed a gun directly at her heart.

Her hold on sanity began to slip.

Sweet heavens! Was he going to kill her?

Trembling panic slammed into her legs, her arms, and her body.

"Please don't make this difficult," Jacob said.

"I'm not going back! You'll just have to shoot me!"

She took a step backward. Warm ocean water swirled around her ankles.

His frown deepened.

Suddenly he reached out and grabbed her arm, jerking her against his muscular length.

"Why did you run, Hannah?"

A tortured look of betrayal flooded his eyes as he glared at her. Instinctively she knew the sweet, gentle Jacob from her teenage years was gone, replaced by a cold, angry man.

A man she could no longer trust.

The thought frightened her, made her panic. With a sudden burst of energy, Hannah slammed the palm of her hand under and up against his chin.

The defensive maneuver worked.

He groaned in surprise, and his tight grasp loosened enough to allow her to wrench free.

In a split second, she was running down the beach. There was no way she was going back to Simon and the Breeder life. No way she would allow men to fuck her until she was pregnant.

From behind her, Jacob yelled at her to stop.

In defiance, her legs moved faster. The thought of him shooting her in the back urged her inland. Forced her to falter over the sharp rocks and to skirt the sand dunes as she headed toward the deserted beach highway. Maybe she'd get lucky and someone would come along. Maybe she could flag someone down before her Hitman flashed his badge.

Unfortunately, the terrain only got rougher, the rocks turned into boulders that were hidden by tall clumps of dry yellow grass.

She stubbed her toe. Pain lanced up her foot into her leg. She bit back a cry, pushed aside the agony, and kept her feet pounding the hard ground.

Her lungs began to burn, her leg muscles cramped, but the pain was nothing compared to the horrors waiting for her when he took her back. Back to a life without freedom.

That thought made her run even faster, if that were possible.

Now she was running at a dangerous pace. Anything could happen. She could hit another boulder, stick her foot into a hole, break a leg....

She could hear his heavy breathing behind her. Could hear the way his shoes pounded the hard, dry earth.

God! He was gaining on her. She could almost feel his hot breath on the back of her neck. Could feel his body heat slam into her flesh.

Sensing he was about to tackle her, she turned abruptly and headed east back toward the beach. She would dive into the ocean. Swim to freedom if she had to.

Behind her, he cursed.

She began to pray like she'd never prayed before. Prayed he would give up. Prayed he would simply let her go.

Her prayers went unanswered.

An instant later, a strong hand grabbed her by the elbow, making her whirl around.

Losing her balance, she fell.

He came down on her like a sack of potatoes, wiping the wind out of her burning lungs.

She couldn't move. Couldn't breathe. Couldn't gather her senses.

He lay on top of her, his hot breath wheezing over her face like erotic caresses. His muscular length seductively grinded her body into the ground. And his dead black eyes glared angrily into her very soul.

"It's over, Hannah. It's over," he breathed.

Over?

It couldn't be over. Not like this. Not here. Not when she was so close to freedom.

Her mind searched frantically for a way out. A way to save herself.

"You can't take me back there! You can't!" Hysteria edged her voice, but through the panic she saw something powerful flash in his eyes.

Was it sympathy? Confusion?

No.

It was desire. Dark and dangerous desire.

The passion in his gaze stunned her. Frightened her. Excited her.

Air ebbed back into her lungs.

Along with her breath came her senses.

All of her senses.

She shouldn't be noticing anything about him. Not after all these years, but she couldn't help it. Not with his hard body pinned so intimately on top of hers. Not with those strong muscular thighs straddling each side of her hips. Nor could she ignore the large masculine knot blossoming against her lower abdomen.

"I've waited so long for you, Hannah. So goddamn long. And when I came home, you were gone."

His eyes didn't seem dead anymore. They flashed with desire and intent. To her shock her body responded to his heated look with a fantastic pleasure of its own.

She wanted to stop the delicious way his powerful chest heaved against her clothing, scraping her nipples. Hardening them into two aching buds of need.

She wanted to deny the pure craving exploding between her legs, but when his hot mouth suddenly dropped against her trembling lips she could do nothing but submit to his seductive assault.

His mouth tasted moist, lusty, and full of secret promises. His lips slid erotically over hers, igniting crisp sparks of want deep into her very core.

She whimpered as his determined tongue slid between her teeth and invaded her mouth.

Unimaginable sensations bombarded her as his hot tongue explored her cavern. Instinctively, she wound her arms around his neck, pulling him closer and her deeper into the intoxicating kiss.

Excitement zipped along her nerve endings making her entire body ache for his touch. Her nipples hardened into tight beads, and a hot wetness seeped from her desire-swollen cunt.

When he finally drew away from her, his face was flushed with want. The thick bulge pressed against her abdomen was thick and hard, making her shiver with a fierce want she'd never experienced before.

"I have to taste you, Hannah. I have to see if you are real."

Her heart crashed in her ears as she concentrated on what he was saying to her.

"I promise I won't hurt you. Just a taste of your sweetness. Just a taste."

Mesmerized by the sexual heat in his eyes, she found herself nodding.

Upon her consent his chest lifted off hers, and he slithered down between her legs. When his hot hands seared against the burning flesh of her inner thighs she fully understood what he wanted to do to her.

The thought that she was about to experience one of those fascinating rumors that had circulated about Jacob back at the Breeding Plantation made the demanding need brew stronger deep in her cunt. It was a shocking heat, an intense yearning for a man she'd never been able to have.

She inhaled sharply as her shorts and underwear were tugged down and off her legs. She felt the warmth of the grainy sand nestle against her ass.

Hannah found herself lifting her knees and spreading her legs for him. She loved the ravenous look brewing in his dark blue eyes. It was a look she remembered so well.

A look he'd never acted on, until now.

But did she want him this way?

Laying half naked on the beach where anyone might witness

what he was about to do to her?

"Jacob...."

"Oh God, you're so beautiful," he whispered from his position between her widespread legs. He looked drunk. Drunk with desire.

Hannah bit back a gasp of pleasure as his hot fingers slid along her inner thighs toward her aching need. She jolted as his fingers parted her nether lips. The stubble on his face grazed against her inner thighs creating a firestorm of longing deep inside her womb. His hot tongue flicked against her pouting pleasure bud, and she couldn't help but moan wantonly.

She closed her eyes and lifted her hips, pressing her aching flesh against his face. Wetness trickled from between her legs as she craved him. Craved for him to be the one and only man who would ever thrust his strong thick shaft deep inside her.

With tormenting licks his tongue explored the crevice of her clit. Over and over he suckled, bit gently and probed roughly until her thighs were shuddering and her body was writhing beneath his hot mouth.

"Jacob, please." Frustration gnawed at her, and she dug her fingers into the warm sand.

She wanted him to fuck her. To bring her to fulfillment. But the words just wouldn't come out of her mouth.

His head lifted, and the powerful drunken look of desire made her heart sing with joy.

"You taste even better than I ever imagined, Hannah. So much sweeter."

She cried out as two long fingers plunged into her heated wetness, and he began to thrust wildly. A thumb frayed erotically over her pleasure nub, and Hannah found herself moaning under his violent onslaught. Moaning until her sensitive insides exploded with an orgasm so intense it took her breath away and made her shudder brutally.

When she began to descend from the pleasure high, his head once again dropped between her legs.

This time his hard long tongue replaced his fingers, burning a line right up her vagina forcing her aroused muscles to clamp around his hot flesh. A calloused thumb swiped against her swollen pleasure nub, rubbing lazy circles until she cried out with the urge to climax.

Greedily, he sucked and sipped at her cunt. His hot mouth brought her to the edge of a precipice she ached to descend into, leaving her gasping for air and her body exquisitely tense.

When she thought she could stand the sweet agony no longer, he slid his tongue out and slipped two fingers inside her wet channel beginning a fast pump. Within seconds, violent shudders pulsed through her, sending her hips crashing against his wild thrusts and her mind falling into a yawning chasm of intense pleasure. It was almost painful. By the time he was finished with her, she lay spent and drained in the sand.

Drained and wanting more from him.

Wanting so much more.

She opened her eyes and saw the sweet drunk look of desire slowly fade away, replaced by that cold dead glare she dreaded.

When he saw her watching him, he gazed away as if ashamed of what he'd just done to her.

But he shouldn't be ashamed. She'd loved the way his hot tongue had seduced her clit. Loved the way his fingers had plunged inside her cunt. Most of all she loved the sparks of desire she'd seen brewing in his eyes when he'd gazed at her.

The mere thought of any other man looking at her like that made desperation flood her senses.

"Jacob, please don't take me back to the Plantation. You can do anything you want to me. Anything. Just don't take me back there," she whispered.

"Anything?"

"Whatever you want."

Her voice didn't give away the fact that her insides quivered frantically. She'd always wanted Jacob but not like this.

"Let's go to my car," he instructed.

"No. Here. You do whatever you want to me here. Then you leave. You let me go."

She held her breath as he gazed down between her spread naked legs. Strangely enough, she didn't feel the least bit ashamed.

Why should she?

Deep in her heart she knew Jacob Romero was a good man. At least he had been before he'd left the Breeding Plantation to become a Hitman. She could only hope he still had some compassion left inside him.

"I want a bed and twenty-four hours," he whispered.

Oh my Goodness! He was taking her up on her offer!

If she thought her limbs were shaking before, they were spastic now.

Twenty-four hours? But what about her rescue boat to the Free

States? It was coming today.

Anxiety raged inside her.

If she didn't go with him, Jacob would see her rescue coming in the boat. He'd find out about the Underground Railway. He'd capture her would-be rescuers. It would ruin the chances for others coming after her.

Hannah tried hard not to turn her head toward the ocean. Toward freedom.

Instead, she locked her gaze onto Jacob who now studied her face.

Did he know? Did he know she was meeting with the Underground Railway?

Oh God! She needed to get him away from here.

Sleeping with him was the only way out. She had to do it. She had to trust he would let her go afterwards.

Reluctantly, Hannah nodded.

Jacob hoisted his powerful body off her, and he kneeled between her legs. To her surprise, he reached down, and his long fingers intertwined with her own.

"Your twenty-four hours start when we get to a hotel." Inwardly she shivered. His words and his warm touch screamed pleasure through her veins as he helped her to her feet. She found herself realizing that her dream of sleeping with Jacob was about to come true. She just hadn't figured it to be this way.

Chapter Two

He was insane. Totally crazy.

Or maybe he was in love?

No, not love. Lust.

He was lusting after a woman he had no business lusting after.
She was a Breeder Slave. A runner.

He was a Hitman. A killer.

They were from two different worlds.

But that hadn't prevented him at the tender age of eighteen from
being friendly with her at his father's Breeding Plantation. It
hadn't prevented him from being sexually attracted to her or from
wanting to claim her for his very own.

God. She'd been the sweetest girl. The only girl he'd really
wanted to fuck. The only girl who had been off-limits.

He'd even asked his father to consider releasing Hannah from
pre-Breeder Slave status so he could claim her for his own.

His father had shook his head in shock. A Plantation owner's
son did not take a Breeder Slave for a wife. It was unheard of. It
was scandalous to even think such a horrid thing.

The next day Jacob had been shipped off to Hitman School. He
hadn't even had a chance to say good-bye to her. Hadn't had a
chance to tell her he wanted her. That he would come back for her
someday.

When his father's message had come informing him of
Hannah's first Breeding Ceremony giving Jacob his blessing to
fuck her, it had been all too bittersweet. His father had given the
same blessing to all his brothers.

He'd secured some time off and come home to demand he be
the first in line to fuck Hannah. Being the eldest son, he had that
right.

But when he'd come home, Hannah was gone.

Escaped.

A goddamn runner.

A runner who wasn't a sweet girl anymore. She was all grown
up.

And he was in trouble.

One beautiful Breeder Slave had gotten under his skin. One taste of her, and he'd been hooked. She'd tasted better than he'd ever imagined.

All sweet and cinnamony. And the musical cries of her aroused whimpers as she climaxed ... Jacob couldn't help but groan inwardly as he remembered the way her hips had thrust her drenched cunt into his face encouraging him to sip more of her heavenly juices.

She was one hell of a sexy woman. Even now as she sat beside him stiff as a corpse body, he could feel the sexual energy pour out of her and over him.

Her full breasts heaved seductively with her every inhalation. Her lush mouth was set in grim determination.

She would do anything he wanted, she'd said.

And he'd accepted her offer.

Oh man. What had he done?

He couldn't even look at himself in the rearview mirror. If he did, he'd see the truth flashing in his eyes.

From the first time he'd seen her long black hair framing a heart-shaped face, red, pouty rosebud lips and slanted green eyes, not to mention the seductive as sin plump body, he'd wanted to claim her.

And now he had her.

Instead of feeling happy, he felt anxious.

She should be dead now. Dead on the beach.

She wasn't. Simply because he hadn't had the heart to do his job.

He'd never had a problem pulling the trigger in the past. Not until now.

Damn!

Instead of doing his job, he'd walked down to the beach with full intentions of warning her of the danger she was in by staying at the deserted mansion.

But the closer he'd gotten to her, the more he wanted to taste her.

To make love to her.

To free her.

Oh man!

The Hitman Association would kill him when they found out what he'd done. And what he was about to do.

Strangely enough, he didn't care what they did to him. Not anymore.

He had Hannah, and he was taking her to God only knew where.

When he'd first spotted her two weeks ago hiding in the deserted mansion, he should have simply walked away. Let someone else do the kill job. But he didn't want her dead. He just wanted her.

Lying on top of her on the beach after he'd tackled her had sealed his fate and hers as well.

He needed to make love to her. Needed to taste every part of her body. Needed to sink his hard, aching rod deep into her warm welcome cunt.

He wanted to feel again. To feel like a man. To forget he was a killing machine.

He should apologize for frightening her.

But he wouldn't do it. Couldn't.

At least not yet.

He needed her to be afraid of him. It would keep her in line.

"I think I'm going to be sick." Her soft voice broke into his thoughts.

He wasn't surprised. "I'll pull over."

She nodded numbly, her hand clamped over her luscious mouth.

He whipped the car off the two lane highway and onto a dirt road lined with pine trees. A moment later they entered a small clearing.

She pushed the door open even before the car had rolled to a stop.

He grimaced as she bent over and wretched. The sound was hollow and ugly.

A memory zipped through his brain. A memory of when he was young and wild. Memories of the endless fucking parties with his father's Breeder Slaves. Memories of the slaves wretching when they'd become pregnant from his seed....

Shit! He shouldn't think about it. He should shove those memories right out of his mind. Pretend they were nightmares, not reality.

What he needed was a good stiff drink. Needed to get himself stone cold drunk and forget everything.

On suddenly shaky legs, he climbed out of the car and inhaled the fresh pine scented air.

Lifting his head, he winced at the intense confusion brewing in Hannah's eyes. She wiped the back of her hand across her delicious looking mouth and watched warily as he approached.

"Are you okay?" he asked.

Her eyes widened in disbelief, and then an angry red blush whipped across her cheeks.

"I told you, I'll do anything you want. But I have to hear you say you'll let me go after we have sex. I need to believe I can trust your word. That you are still an honorable man."

Honorable man?

If he was so honorable, he'd be telling her the truth. That he hadn't been able to stop thinking about her since the day he'd left home.

The desperation in her eyes forced him to lie, "I give you my word."

"Then take me. Now. We can do it in the back seat."

He felt his jaw open in surprise.

Felt the guilt at wanting to fuck her take over. He could still taste the sweetness of her cunt juices in his mouth. Oh, he wanted her. Wanted her so much he didn't think his whole body and mind had ever hurt so bad for a woman.

"I won't touch you. Not if you don't want me to," he found himself saying.

Now it was her turn to be surprised. The fear in her eyes diminished, replaced by a sparkle of hope.

"What are you saying? Are you letting me go?"

"No."

She bit her bottom lip, and he saw the tears bubble up in those gorgeous green eyes.

"Dammit! Don't cry," he snapped harshly.

"You've changed your mind, haven't you? You're taking me back to the Breeding Plantation, aren't you?"

"No."

"What do you want from me?"

"I want to make love to you." The words escaped his mouth before he could stop them.

A frown burrowed between her dark eyebrows.

"You just said if I don't want to...."

"I don't want just sex. I want you," he said.

She blinked at him.

He cursed softly at the god-awful confusion etching her face and reached into his back pocket for the item stashed there.

"Here." He unwrapped a stick of pine gum and held it out to her.

She took it and put it in her seductive mouth. God, what he wouldn't do to have her warm lips kissing his aching shaft. Sucking his hot flesh.

He shook the erotic thoughts away.

"I'm going to make a call," he instructed, "I'm keeping an eye on you, so stay right here."

She winced at his harsh tone, and he cursed himself for being so gruff with her.

Keeping an eye on her, he made his way back to the car. From his glove compartment, he dug out his cell phone and dialed the number.

His father's secretary answered and put Jacob straight through to his dad.

"Jacob! How the hell are you?"

"Cut the pleasantries, dad."

His father's voice immediately sobered. "Is she dead?"

"She ran when she saw me." At least that wasn't a lie.

His father cursed a long line of blue words that made Jacob wince.

"I thought they taught you better in that damn Hit School, boy!"

"I'm in hot pursuit."

Jacob watched Hannah as she leaned over and used her fingertips to comb out the tangles in her long black hair. Man, what he wouldn't do to be able to thrust his fingers through those silky strands. To feel their softness flood his palms.

"Did you hear what I said?"

"What?"

"I said it's urgent she's removed."

"Why can't I just bring her home?" The mere suggestion of returning her to him made sour bile bite the back of his throat.

"I want her dead. She's humiliated your brothers and me. Not to mention you and the ten other male Breeder Slaves who were hopefuls for her second child. Just kill her! You know what'll happen to you if you don't."

There it was. The warning.

Get the hit. Or get hit. The Hitman's code of honor stating a Hitman would die before ever giving up a hit.

"I'll call when the job is done," Jacob said between clenched teeth. He pressed the End button on the phone.

Quickly he entered another number.

He sighed in relief when a familiar man's voice answered on the first ring.

"I'm in deep shit, Tool. Really deep shit," Jacob blurted.

The man on the other line chuckled. "What else is new? What happened this time? You smash up the company car? They short change your pay check again?"

Jacob drew in a deep breath and almost revealed his problem. Almost confessed that he had his hit right here, and he wasn't going to kill her.

Deep in his heart he sensed he could trust Tool with the truth. But he just couldn't take the chance. It was better that he trusted no one. Not even his best friend.

It was safer for Hannah.

"My hit saw me. She ran."

"Are you shitting me? You're losing your touch, bud. So, what do you need?"

"I need twenty-four hours of down time. No interruptions what so ever. I've found a willing woman, and we need some privacy. When I'm relaxed, I'll go after the hit who got away," he lied.

"Well shit! It's about time! Haven't I told you fucking a willing woman is the only way to relax? Christ, you Plantation boys are so damned stubborn. You guys just don't listen to me. The fucking is much sweeter when you work for it. What is it that you need?"

"I need you to turn off the tracker in my car."

"What?"

"You heard me."

Tool's tone turned wary. "You know I'm not supposed to do that."

"Can you do it anyway? Divert my whereabouts. Keep it between us?"

"Must be some woman."

"She is."

Silence on the other end. He could almost hear Tool's mind grinding with curiosity.

A moment later his friend's curse of defeat wafted over the line.

"I don't like this."

"Thanks, Tool."

"Twenty-four hours?"

"Twenty-four hours."

"Consider it done. I'll call you when you're times up," Tool said, and he disconnected.

Jacob stuffed the phone into the glove compartment and eased back out of the car.

When he turned around, he froze.

Hannah stood right there. Not more than two feet from him.

Uncertainty filled her green eyes. A somewhat wobbly smile was plastered on her rosy lips.

His gaze lowered. His eyes widened.

Sweet shit! This cannot be happening. And yet it was.

She stood before him.

A goddess.

A very naked goddess.

His greedy gaze raked over her voluptuous figure. A waist that curved inward, hips and breasts that curved outward giving her body an hourglass look. Hungrily he scanned her shapely legs to the dark curly haired muff hiding her wonderful clit from his view.

His shaft sprang to life. Heated like molten steel. Hardened into an iron bar.

He remembered the delicate taste of her cunt. The soft hot feel of her pulsing pleasure nub against his mouth as he'd drained her sweetness from her cavern.

Mouth suddenly dry, he swept his gaze over her slightly rounded abdomen, to her cute little belly button, her satiny belly and finally up.

To his disappointment her silky black hair hid those full breasts from his view.

Jacob let out a ragged breath.

He should tell her to cover herself. Should tell her to run. To get away from him.

But he could say nothing. He could do nothing. Do nothing but stand there and hover at this dangerous line between wanting her and doing what was right by her.

"Jacob?" She said softly.

"Don't do this, Hannah...."

He cursed beneath his breath as she took a step forward.

What the hell was she doing? He'd already told her she didn't have to have sex with him.

She took another step closer.

He took one step back.

The wobbly smile on her pretty face turned into one of curiosity as she tilted up one corner of her lip.

Her eyes were hot with blatant desire as her gaze slid over his face. Before he knew it, she stood right there in front of him. Barely a foot apart.

He breathed in her scent. She smelled fresh and salty like the ocean. A hint of the pine gum she'd been chewing wafted into his nostrils.

Desire rumbled through him. He needed to touch her. Needed to show her he'd never hurt her.

With trembling hands, he reached out.

She inhaled softly as he parted the veil of her silky black hair to reveal swollen breasts with plump pink nipples.

His legs watered. His self-control wavered.

He forced himself to close his eyes in an effort to gather the strength he needed to keep himself from touching her.

"Don't look away," she breathed.

Her hand came up, and she cupped his chin. The gentle touch of her warm fingers against his skin made him groan.

Her body heat cradled him. Made him wish she was his forever.

He trembled as her other hand dipped inside his pants. Her fingers splayed flat against his belly. Only inches from his rock-hard cock. He felt his erection growing in anticipation.

"You don't have to do this, Hannah," he croaked.

"Yes, I do."

"Why?"

"Because ... I want to. I've wanted to for a long time."

Oh man!

Her electric fingers slid around his hard shaft. Her hot touch made him harden violently. Made his sensitive flesh ache with a raging heat. A need that shattered his self control.

Roughly, he grabbed her by her bare shoulders. The silkiness of her velvety skin seared against his fingertips. Her warm minty breath cascaded against his cheeks. Drowned his senses.

Her hand urged his chin towards her luscious trembling lips.

This couldn't be happening. This had to be another dark fantasy. Another fantasy in an endless string of them.

"Hannah?"

"Shhhh." Her breath washed warm and minty against his face.

Oh boy, this was real.

The impact of her soft mouth upon his lips devastated him. It hurled him into another world. A world of a pleasure so intense he had to harden his hold on her shoulders or surely he would fall to his knees.

Her hand uncapped his chin as she deepened the kiss. His world tilted awkwardly. His breath caught in his lungs. His mouth anxiously opened wider allowing her sweet tongue to enter.

She kissed him greedily, her burning mouth cruelly demanding. Her fierce masterful strokes clashed with his tongue creating such a wrenching desire deep in his soul he literally felt the coldness encasing his heart begin to melt.

Her other hand slid under his shirt and over the tight muscles of his chest. He inhaled sharply as she tweaked his sensitive nipples. Ripples of longing sent heated blood roaring to parts south. His shaft throbbed, and a wild fever set through the rest of his body.

A guttural moan started somewhere deep in his chest and

somehow got lost in his throat as her fingers slid sweetly along the entire length of his hard shaft.

Have mercy! It had been so long since he'd been with a woman. So long since he'd been stroked with such tenderness. So long that her mere touch was going to make him come any second.

But he wanted to be inside her when he did. Wanted to feel her velvety muscles clamp around him as she welcomed him deep inside her warmth.

When her hand left his nipple and headed toward the area beneath his arm, the area where he kept his gun holstered, a wiggle of warning whispered in his ear.

Shit!

He should have known. He should have known she was only using him!

Before her hand could curl around his gun, he forced himself to rip his mouth free from her tormenting sweetness.

A tiny cry of protest escaped through her slightly parted lips. The hot look in her eyes flared with disappointment.

"You're good, Hannah. Real good."

"What's wrong? I thought...."

"You thought you could keep me amused so you could go for my gun, and I was stupid enough to fall for it."

A brief look of shame flittered across her face. A look that didn't sit right with her natural beauty.

For a split second, he believed she had wanted him to fuck her. But that would only be wishful thinking.

She looked away, her face flaming pink with embarrassment.

Dammit!

He should take her. Lean her over the hood of the car and just slide his throbbing cock into her. Right here. Right now.

It sure as hell would ease the ache in his hard shaft. Yet he couldn't do it. Couldn't take advantage of her like this.

"Get dressed," he ordered.

At the sound of the harshness in his voice, he felt better. Felt more in control.

She moved away from him but not before he saw the tears glisten in her eyes.

"Hannah!"

She stopped.

"Don't do that again. Not unless you really mean it. Next time I won't stop. Next time I'll fuck you so hard, you'll be begging me to never stop."

He didn't miss the tremor zip through her body. Was she scared of his warning? Or had that been a shiver of excitement?

He watched her get dressed. Her movements graceful. Seductive. Damned arousing.

The thought of going into the woods and jerking himself off entered his mind. But he didn't. He couldn't afford to be out of her sight for too long.

When she was dressed, he grabbed her by the arm and hauled her to the other side of the car where the passenger door stood open.

"Get in the car, Hannah."

"You've changed Jacob. You used to be kind and gentle. Now you're just a cold bastard."

Before he could say anything, she broke free from his grasp, slumped into the car, and slammed the door shut with such a force it hurt his ears.

She kept silent as he started the car and drove out of the secluded area onto the main road.

It was going to be the silent treatment, was it?

He could easily break that silence. He'd have her screaming out with pleasure before too long. Then maybe when he got her out of his system, he'd finally be able to let her go.

Chapter Three

Hannah jolted awake. For a minute she had no idea where she was.

The feeling wasn't uncommon. Not with the way she'd been on the run the past few weeks. Every night a new place to sleep. Every day watching over her shoulder to see if someone followed her.

Now as she peered out the side car window, she blinked at the semi-darkness of twilight enveloping the fast moving landscape of rolling hills and tried to remember what had happened.

A split second later, it all came crashing around her like a horrible landslide.

Jacob had caught her! Jacob the Hitman.

A seemingly cold bastard on the outside and yet when his body had covered hers on the beach, something wild and lusty had been unleashed inside her. When his hot tongue had scooped against her clit as he devoured her, she'd melted like liquid silver, her body betraying her with a powerful lust she couldn't ignore.

Hannah shivered involuntarily when she remembered pursuing him in the meadow.

She'd been desperate. Hadn't been thinking clearly.

The thought of being so close to freedom down at the beach and having it slip through her fingers had screwed her common sense. Had made her queasy and sick to her stomach.

She'd wanted him to fuck her. So he would let her go.

But when she'd approached him in the meadow, he'd backed away from her. Fear had shone in his eyes. Fear and confusion.

Why was he scared of her?

Why would he agree to the proposition of her allowing him to do whatever he wanted to do to her and then just change his mind?

If he was afraid of her, why should she be afraid of him?

Much needed confidence had flooded through her giving her the idea to go after his gun. And the only way to do that was to distract him.

When she'd kissed him, his searing warmth had curled through her body, pushing aside any remaining fear. And when he'd returned her kiss ... it was as if an electrical field had encompassed them. A wild energy that zapped through her entire being awakening all her senses into full alert.

His thick arousal had pressed intimately against her suddenly wet and eager cunt.

God help her, she'd wanted him to bury his hot flesh deep inside her. To make her forget all her troubles. To make her remember why she'd liked him so much when they'd been younger. And best of all, he'd made her feel safe. Safe and secure from the outside world.

But when he'd broken the kiss and accused her of trying to steal his gun, she'd been stunned. She'd been unable to comprehend why lust had overwhelmed her so much for a man she hadn't seen in so long.

Hannah closed her eyes, blocking out the memories.

Why in heaven's name had she come onto him in the meadow?

Because she'd had to, that's why. Getting his gun was the only way to escape.

But what would happen when she got the gun? She had no idea how to use one.

"There's a hotel up ahead," his voice snapped through her thoughts. "There's a restaurant too, if you're hungry."

"I'm not hungry."

He said nothing as he took the exit.

A shiver ripped through Hannah as she watched him. His full mouth pouted. His handsome face determined.

Had he changed his mind? Was he going to tell her the deal was still on? He'd said the deal would start when they reached the hotel. Is that why he hadn't wanted to make love to her in the meadow?

Her stomach tightened with dread.

Or was it anticipation?

Christ, she wasn't horny.

Just scared shitless. And desperate.

But if she was scared, why was she anxious to feel his warm lips sliding against hers again. Why did she want to feel his silk encased steel thick rod throbbing in her hand again? And why was she hoping he would bring back those feelings of pleasure? Of feeling safe in his arms.

He pulled into the hotel parking lot.

The hotel was a small one-story building. A bit run down. But small and quaint. Surrounded by a large meadow at the sides and a string of tiny pine trees along the front lawn.

He turned to her. "Let's go inside and register. You make any moves to escape or draw any attention to us, our agreement is off. I'll have no choice but to send you straight back to the Breeding Plantation."

Oh God! The deal was still on!

Hannah held her breath as she climbed out of the car and followed him into the lobby.

The lobby smelled of freshly brewed coffee and stale cigarette smoke. The lobby clerk was an older gray haired gentleman who set down the newspaper he'd been reading when he saw them and greeted them enthusiastically.

Hannah bit her lips against the scream building inside her as Jacob spoke with the lobby clerk. Anxiety mounted when she saw him hand the clerk some cash.

She forced herself to inhale slowly. To stay calm.

He wouldn't hurt her. She had to believe that. He'd always been kind to her in the past. Had always been friendly.

And she'd always wanted Jacob....

Excitement mingled with dread.

He could do whatever he wanted to her in the hotel room and still not let her go.

He turned around, and, to her surprise, he held out a roll of antacids. He must have picked it up at the counter.

"For your stomach."

He was concerned for her health? Confusion gripped her guts, and she accepted the roll.

"Room 13. To the left and on the end," he said.

He waved her ahead of him out the door.

The urge to bolt was great. So great she almost ran. But she knew he was watching her.

She could feel the heat of his laser sharp eyes on her back. If she ran, he'd catch her in a split second.

He'd be angry. He'd probably cuff her. Then he could do with her whatever he wanted. He had every right, too. His father owned her for God's sake. And when he was finished with her, he'd send her back.

Her stomach sank at the thought of returning to the Plantation. Back to the other Breeder Slaves who would laugh at her, taunt her for getting caught. Back to the rowdy Romero brothers who would fuck her endlessly just like they did the other Breeder Slaves.

She had better do what Jacob wanted. She had to keep him

happy. Satisfied. Hopefully he would keep his word and let her go.

The door to room 13 swung inward, and Hannah stepped inside. Quickly, she scanned the room for an escape route. A bathroom was nestled in the back corner.

A bathroom always contained a window. She'd wait until he slept and pretend she was going to the bathroom and climb out the window.

"Cozy little room," he said from behind her and flicked on the lights.

"Perfect." She managed a weak smile as she spied the cozy double bed in the middle of the room. A pretty pink comforter covered it. On the wall above the bed hung a giant heart shaped picture frame depicting a man and a woman holding hands as they walked through a dandelion strewn meadow.

Freedom screamed out of the picture, and Hannah found herself tensing up with anxiety again.

If Jacob hadn't come when he had, she'd be on the boat to freedom now.

Yet if he hadn't come, she would never have seen him again.

Sadness tugged at her heart. She wasn't sure if it was because of the thought of never seeing Jacob again or of losing her freedom.

"You sure you're not hungry?"

"Food is the last thing on my mind," Hannah replied.

He scowled.

He'd been frowning since he'd finished doing her on the beach. Was he sorry for pleasuring her? Or was it because he didn't know if he should let her go?

Hannah inhaled softly as she remembered the old Jacob.

Before he'd left to be a Hitman, he'd always had a smile on his face for her. She wondered what had happened to him. Wondered what kinds of things he'd had to do as a Hitman.

Her heart wrenched at the self-conscious way he thrust his hand through his silky brown hair.

"Listen, what I said in the hotel lobby... about sending you back to the Breeding Plantation. I just didn't want you causing a scene."

Relief soared through her at his softly spoken words.

"If you have to go to the bathroom, go now. Leave the door open."

"So you can watch? I don't think so."

"Leave the door open or don't go. I won't watch."

"I don't have to go."

"Lie down on the bed then."

"What?"

"Lie down."

Oh God, he was going to start now.

Shakily, Hannah went over to the side of the bed closest to the bathroom and sat on the lumpy mattress.

He watched her as she lay down, then he crawled onto the bed beside her.

He was a big man. A muscular man. Definitely not that gangly eighteen year old she'd innocently flirted with before he'd abruptly left for school.

If they'd been two other people ... met in some other way, they might have had a chance at something special.

"Just relax, Hannah. You're safe. For now."

Hannah's heart began to pound with anxiety.

"What's that supposed to mean?"

He ignored her question. "Give me your hand."

"What?"

"Either give me your hand, or I'll have to slap on the cuffs."

She held out her hand, and he laced his fingers intimately with hers, holding her tight.

The warmth from his hands sunk deep into her flesh, branding her. Making her come alive with those lovely sensations she just wasn't used to.

With his other hand he reached out and flicked off the lamp on the night table. The room plunged into darkness.

Immediately his rich masculine scent swarmed all over her, resurrecting the memories of today. Making her remember the crisp feel of his chest hairs beneath her fingertips as she'd pinched his pebble-hard nipples. The hot satiny feel of his skin and the underlying rigid stomach muscles.

His sexy scent had been her aphrodisiac, urging her on. The electricity springing up through her body as she'd touched his skin had made her fingers boldly wrap around the hot flesh of his thick penis.

The pulsing heat and power throbbing against her fingers had been awesome. Heat had flooded throughout her body. Thick and hot. Most of it settling low in her belly. Leaving her body and her senses blazing with uncontrollable want.

She'd wanted his hot body pinning her against the cold metal of his car. Wanted to feel the thick power of his fiery erection deep inside her as he slammed into her cunt in a desperate effort to put out the erotic ache he'd created between her legs.

"Why did you run, Hannah?" His rough voice broke her from her thoughts.

She blinked wildly into the darkness. The unexpected question stunned her. It made her remember the last night she'd been with Simon. Made her remember the helplessness enveloping her when he'd told her she was going to her first Breeding Ceremony the next morning. Desperation had flooded her at the thought of so many men being set loose upon her.

She remembered the endless complaints from the other Breeder Slave women when they'd gone through their own first Ceremony. How tired and sore they'd been trying to accommodate so many men. How happy they'd been to learn they were finally pregnant and would have some months of peace and quiet. But that still hadn't stopped the men from coming to them. It had slowed some of them down, but after the baby was born it would start all over again.

"I don't want to be a Breeder Slave," she blurted out.

"My father purchased you for that purpose. You're his property. He can do with you what he pleases."

"No man owns me."

She flinched as his fingers tightened around hers.

"Who the hell taught you this crap? You're mother?"

"She taught me plenty before she died. Every time she gave birth and was forced to give a child away to strangers, it broke her heart. Every time the men hounded her before and after she became pregnant, it made her sad. Life without love, she said, was not a life worth living. Before she died she made me promise to get away before I became designated a slave, too. She made me realize I don't have to go through hell just because some man bought me."

Beside her Jacob sighed heavily. "You've embarrassed the family. They're very upset."

"I'm sorry for their pain." She truly was. The Romero's had been kind to her.

Jacob's father had taught her some pleasures of lovemaking. He'd been gentle with her. Brought her to climax many times with his fingers and a dildo, but she wanted more out of life. She wanted to experience the rumors of being in a monogamous relationship.

She wanted a man's love, not just sex.

She wanted her freedom.

Jacob didn't say anything, but his fingers loosened their grip ever so slightly around hers. Despite her best efforts to stop it, the intimate gesture sparked more arousal to course through her veins.

"Go to sleep, Hannah," he said wearily.

Reluctantly, Hannah closed her eyes.

Today's meadow adventure came swiftly to mind. She remembered the intimate way his thick arousal had pressed desperately against the apex of her legs while she'd kissed him.

She'd never been sexually aggressive in her life. Not until today in the meadow with Jacob.

Now that she'd crossed the line, she wasn't sure if she could stop herself from doing it again.

* * * *

Jacob opened his eyes to find Hannah standing in the semi-darkness beside the bed looking down at him. Her hands cupped her naked breasts, and she held them out to him in a blatant offer.

Carnal thoughts speared through his brain at the sensual sight.

His breathing quickened. His cock hardened into a searing band of molten steel.

"What are you doing, Hannah?" he managed to croak.

"Giving us what we both want."

"You don't have to do this, Hannah. Not for me."

"I want you. I want your mouth all over me. I want you inside me."

She pressed her silky breasts closer to his face. They heaved gently with every breath. They tempted him like he'd never been tempted before.

His mouth watered as his gaze zeroed in on her large nipples.

Have mercy. How the hell could he resist such a delicious offer?

He licked his lips in anticipation and leaned forward, placing a teasing kiss at the tip of one plump nipple. It was a tight bud. A delicious blossom of warmth.

She moaned erotically.

He smiled and drew the lush nipple into his mouth. Her flesh tasted like sweet nectar and sex.

His tongue teased the tight bud, and she whimpered.

"Make love to me, Jacob. Fuck me hard."

"Oh my dear Hannah. I've wanted you for so long."

She moaned again. It was an animalistic sound.

Too wild. Not at all what Hannah had sounded like when he'd seduced her cunt on the beach or when they'd kissed in the meadow.

A tinge of alarm zipped up his spine, and he stopped suckling.

The moans continued.

What the hell?

Jacob opened his eyes and blinked wildly at the harsh noises drifting through the darkness.

A dream!

Orienting himself, he quickly discovered the sounds weren't coming from Hannah but from the adjoining motel room.

Bed springs squeaked. A man groaned. The woman's harsh moans continued.

Shit!

His cock pulsed at the sounds. Pulsed and tightened into one hell of an aching rod.

He was about to pound on the wall to tell the lovers to quieten down when he realized Hannah was awake beside him.

In the darkness he couldn't see her, but her breathing was shallow, her warm fingers wrapped tightly around his.

"I guess you hear the festivities next door," he whispered.

Her slight inhalation sounded so sexy he wanted to rip her clothes off and plunge himself deep inside her making her cry out with desire.

She didn't say anything for a long time as they both listened to the mating sounds from the couple.

Finally she spoke, "Why didn't you fuck me in the meadow or on the beach and then take me directly back to the Plantation?"

"I'll take you back if you want me to," he lied.

He could never take her back. She wasn't welcome there anymore.

"Is that what you want me to do? To go back? So any man who wants me can have me? Do you think it's right that I don't even have a say in my own destiny? In the past all women were free to do whatever they wanted."

"It's illegal to speak of the past, Hannah."

"Who's going to hear us? Certainly not the couple next door."

The woman's wild moans ripped through the air making Jacob's shaft grow even harder.

"Why did you tell Simon you wanted to participate in my Breeding Ceremony?"

Shit!

"Go back to sleep, Hannah."

"Is that the only way you can get laid? Fucking women during the Breeding Ceremonies?"

"You make it sound so horrible."

"Isn't it?"

"It's the way it is now, Hannah. You know that. Having slaves is the best way to insure a working couple doesn't take time off work to have the kids they want."

"How convenient for them," Hannah snapped.

"Christ, Hannah! You're the first Breeder Slave to run from my father's plantation in thirty years, did you know that? I always figured our Slaves were happy with their lot in life."

"And that's why so many of them escape from other plantations? That's why there's so many Hitmen and Hitgals employed? Because the slaves enjoy their lot in life?"

He could hear the bitterness pouring out of her voice. He wasn't surprised. It was a familiar story. He'd heard it many times from other runners just before he'd pulled the trigger and put a bullet through their brains.

Jacob's stomach heaved at the thought of all the people he'd killed in the name of duty. Killed simply because their owners wanted them dead and the Slaves wanted their freedom. And because he himself was a weak son of a bitch who couldn't go up against the Association and tell them he didn't want anything to do with being a Hitman.

Instead, he'd just gone along with the hand dealt to him. Went along with his own lot in life.

Hell, he didn't deserve to think about having happiness in his life. Didn't deserve to have Hannah lying here on the bed beside him.

The moans from the couple next door grew frenzied, louder.

In response, Hannah tried to jerk her hand away from his grasp.

He wouldn't let her go.

She sighed in frustration.

"I'm sorry about what happened today in the meadow," he whispered, trying to calm her down.

"You said you wanted me, earlier on the beach. Why'd you back off?"

"Because you don't want me," he admitted.

She remained silent for a long time after that. Secretly he'd hoped she would whisper again that she'd wanted him in the past. That she still wanted him.

"Yet you forced me to come with you, even when you know I don't want to have sex with you. Why?"

How the hell did he answer that one? Should he tell her the

truth? Tell her he'd fallen in love with her the moment he'd seen her climb out of his father's truck after he'd brought her to the Plantation? If he told her that, she'd laugh her bloody head off.

"I haven't had sex with a woman in a long time."

Shit, where did that come from?

"And I just happened to be the first woman you've come across that you've wanted to fuck in a long time?"

"Something like that."

She gave a strange little chuckle. "You're just like all the other men."

All the other men?

Anger erupted inside him. Anger at the thought of how close she'd come to being passed around to all his brothers and numerous other men.

"They see a woman's naked body, and they begin to fantasize. Some of them can't even wait until the Ceremonies before they force themselves on a Slave."

"Did a man force himself on you? Did my father force himself?"

"Your father owned me, Jacob. I didn't have much choice in the matter of entertaining him. But I enjoyed the sex training he put me through."

Strangely enough there was no bitterness in her voice. But if she'd said it to wound him, it worked. Nauseau crawled in his guts at the thought of his father and Hannah together.

Beside him, Hannah wiggled around. A moment later, her sweet breath cascaded over his face. He could almost see her silhouette in the darkness. Her face mere inches from his.

"I think you're one of those men who fantasize and don't do anything about it, Jacob. I think you've been fantasizing about me for a long time, haven't you? I remember how you used to look at me. How friendly you were to me. How different you were with me than you were with the other Breeder Slaves. You didn't seem to mind fucking them. But you always kept your distance from me. Back then I thought you didn't want me. But now you say you do. But you've changed, Jacob. Not for the better. What happened to you? Why are your eyes so cold?"

Jacob tensed at her questions.

"What did they do to you in that Hit school?"

"Let it be, Hannah," he warned.

She inhaled a breath and then wiggled away from him.

"I don't think you're planning on ever taking me back to the Plantation, Jacob. Am I right?"

"Be quiet and go to sleep, Hannah."

"I'll be quiet if you tell me the truth. Why are we here? Why aren't we heading back to the Plantation?"

"Because you can't go back there, Hannah. I've been sent here to kill you."

Chapter Four

Her shocked inhalation made him wince. Made him realize she really had no idea how badly she'd hurt the family by running away.

"Are you going to kill me?" she whispered.

"You even have to ask?"

He could hear her breathing deepen in the darkness. And he could hear something else, too. Something besides the erotic moans from the couple next door.

It was a quiet rattling noise that raised the fine hairs on the back of his neck.

Someone was wiggling the doorknob.

For a few breath-taking seconds he lay frozen as a hot slice of betrayal slammed into his guts.

Son of a bitch!

His best friend, Tool, must have alerted the Association about his request and turned the tracking device back on in his car. They must have sent someone to check on him.

If they found Hannah here with him, they'd kill her on the spot.

Trying hard to ignore the raging panic grabbing hold of his senses, Jacob slid the car keys out of his front pants pocket.

"Hannah. Take the keys, climb out the back window, get to the car, and get the hell out of here," he whispered.

"What?"

"Someone's found us."

"What do you mean?" Panic etched her voice. She didn't move.

Tugging on her hand, he pulled her across the bed with him, making her stand up beside him. Slapping the keys into her palm, he slid the gun from his holster.

He kept his voice low as he spoke. "Once you're in the car, I want you to get out of here as casually as you can. Ditch the car the first chance you get. There's a tracker on it. Now, go. Get out of here."

"What about you?"

"I'll be fine. Just go."

She didn't move.

Impatience ripped through Jacob, and he shoved her roughly

toward the bathroom. Quietly, he slid the window open and looked outside.

A blue glaze from the moon drenched the yard, and he had no trouble scanning the emptiness of the motel's yard.

He saw no movement.

When he turned around he saw the fear reflected in her moonlit eyes, and it just about broke his heart. He wished he could give her a good-bye kiss, but there wasn't any time.

"Stay to the right. And whatever happens, don't come back."

"What's wrong?"

"Go," he whispered.

She hesitated just long enough to piss him off. Grabbing her by her waist, he hoisted her to the windowsill and practically shoved her outside.

Then he rushed back into the bedroom and headed for the front door.

* * * *

Hannah held her breath as she eased her way through the moonlit yard to the side of the hotel. Her heart thundered in her ears as she stumbled through the tall weeds that lined a cracked sidewalk.

At the same time her mind tumbled in confusion.

Why was Jacob so afraid? Why had he shoved her out the back window? Why had he told her to get in the car and leave him and not come back?

It didn't make sense. He was a Hitman. He was supposed to be with her. But then again, he said he was supposed to have killed her.

She peeked around to the front of the hotel. Aside from the dim lamps shining onto the parking lot, she didn't see anyone.

Perhaps no one had tried to break in? Maybe Jacob had overreacted?

Maybe she should just get her ass in gear and get into the car and make her escape.

Fiddling with the car keys, she picked out the one she hoped would unlock the door then walked toward Jacob's car where he'd left it parked near the lobby.

Thankfully the car sat only about ten feet away from her, but it seemed like it was an eternity away.

From the opposite end of the hotel where their room was located she heard the sound of two men talking.

Hannah paused at the driver's side of the car and strained her ears in an effort to listen.

"You know it's against policy to have them turn off the tracking devices, Romero," a gruff voice echoed from the open doorway of their room.

"Just wanted some time off to spend with a beautiful woman, Sawblade. I cleared it with Tool," came Jacob's casual reply.

"So where is this beautiful woman?" the man named Sawblade asked.

Hannah inserted the key into the car door slot. The door purred open.

She was about to get in when a man's shout from behind her made her freeze. She didn't dare stop. But her back tingled as she imagined a bullet ripping into her, effectively ending her quest for freedom.

From behind her, hurried footsteps approached.

She dropped into the driver's seat, slid the key into the ignition, and started the car.

Before she could put the car into drive, a gun kissed the window mere inches from her face.

Hannah clamped down the urge to scream.

"Get out of the car, Hannah," the stranger said roughly. God! He knew her name. Knew she was a runner.

Her pulse exploded as he tapped the gun on her window.

"Now!"

Oh God!

"C'mon runner. Get out of the car. I've got big plans for you." The leery grin and the way he tugged at the protruding bulge between his legs informed Hannah exactly what he had in mind for her.

Suddenly the man whirled around, and Hannah glimpsed Jacob a few feet away. His gun was drawn on the stranger.

"She's leaving, Sawblade," Jacob said coldly.

"You're letting your hit go?" Disbelief marred the Hitman's face.

"Get the hell out of here, Hannah!" Jacob yelled at her.

Before Hannah knew what was happening, gunshots rang through the air.

Without hesitation, she slammed her foot onto the accelerator. The car ploughed backward and smashed into another parked car, jarring her forward like a rag doll.

Gathering her senses, she whipped the car into drive. In front of her, Jacob had taken cover behind another parked car, and both men were firing upon each other.

Hannah's heart lodged in her throat when she spotted a dark patch on Jacob's upper left thigh.

Oh my God! He's been hit!

Without thinking, Hannah whipped the car into the parking spot beside Jacob and flung open the passenger door.

He dove in.

Within a split second, she had the car in reverse and flew out of the parking lot.

Hannah screamed, and Jacob cursed as the entire back window exploded sending a shower of glass over them.

A glance into the rear-view mirror showed the Hitman bending over, clutching his belly and gasping for air as he watched them leave.

Then he turned around and limped over to a nearby car, waving at the startled people who had now appeared at their hotel doors.

"Shit! He's coming after us!" Hannah cried.

She watched as the Hitman climbed into a car. The red taillights flicked on.

"He's coming!"

"He's not," Jacob said through deep gasps. His voice was way too casual under the circumstances.

Panic built inside Hannah as she spied the Hitman's car pulling out of the parking lot.

"Oh God! He's coming."

Suddenly the car in the rearview mirror stopped.

Jacob winked at her. "I plugged a couple of bullets into his tires."

"You were that sure I'd come back for you?" She found herself asking as the full impact of what he'd done to the Hitman's tires settled in.

He grinned in answer, and her entire body lurched with pleasure. The feeling was short lived when he winced and leaned his head back against the seat. Her heart stopped at the sight of blood soaking his upper thigh.

"I'll stop a few miles up ahead and check on the bullet wound."

"It's just a flesh wound. Keep going. We have to ditch this car somewhere. We have to hide. Sawblade will report what happened here. We're both on the hit list now."

Sweet mercy, Jacob had put his life on the line for her. What in the world had he been thinking?

"I know where we can hide." Even as the words tumbled out of her mouth she didn't know if she could risk taking Jacob there.

Had he heard the rumors of the deserted mansion? Of how it was a contact point for runaway Breeder Slaves?

"It's okay. I know where. I've been watching you since you hit that deserted mansion two weeks ago."

"What?"

"I watched you go skinny dipping every morning in the ocean and the other things you did."

A strange thrill cascaded through her body at the thought of him watching her.

"I could have taken you anytime. I could have killed you..." He sighed and closed his eyes.

"Why didn't you?" She found herself asking.

Sadness twisted his lips, and he closed his eyes. "I will take you, Hannah. When the time is right, I will make love to you like a man makes love to his woman."

Oh sweet heavens!

"I told you I belong to no man." The words didn't ring true even to her own ears.

"When the time is right you will be mine, Hannah. In every way possible. That's a promise."

The confidence in his voice left little doubt he would follow through with his promise.

To Hannah's surprise, she couldn't wait for that pledge to come true.

* * * *

Jacob must have drifted off.

Subconsciously he realized that fact and came awake with one hell of a jolt. With the wakefulness came the intense pain in his upper thigh and a hot fever burning throughout his body.

It was still dark outside, but through the car window he could see the dim gray streak of dawn brightening the eastern horizon.

"Who's Tool?" she asked as she peered over at him.

Jacob blinked in puzzlement. He didn't remember mentioning his friend, Tool, to her.

When he didn't respond, she explained, "You were saying his name in your sleep."

The ache of betrayal bit deep into his belly.

"Who is he? Another Hitman."

"He was monitoring the tracking devices on our cars, making sure the Association knows our every move. I asked him to turn off the tracker on my car until I could get you somewhere safe. He said he'd do it. I thought I could trust him."

"Personal experience has shown me not to trust anyone," Hannah said.

"Not even me?

"Not even you," she whispered

Ouch.

"You must have trusted me at some point. You came back for me at the hotel when Sawblade had me cornered."

She frowned and didn't say anything.

"Just don't do anything stupid like that again," he warned.

"With a thanks like that, don't expect me to."

Despite the throbbing pain in his thigh, Jacob couldn't help but to chuckle.

"You're very pretty when you're mad, Hannah. I can't wait to see your face wrenched with pure pleasure when I'm thrusting deep inside you."

Her surprised gasp made him smile. He settled back against the passenger seat of his car. Satisfaction gnawed at his bones.

She hadn't protested what he'd just said. Was she warming up to the idea of him making love to her? If so, it was a damn good incentive to get himself better in one hell of a hurry.

* * * *

The first thing Jacob noticed the next time he woke up was that his body wasn't on fire any more. And to his shock, he wasn't in the car anymore.

Instead, he lay on a somewhat lumpy bed in the cozy attic room of the abandoned mansion Hannah had sequestered herself while she'd stayed here.

He knew where he was because he'd stolen into this very room while she'd slept. He'd sat beside the bed watching her naked breasts rise and fall in the moonlight. Hungered for a taste of the sweetness she harbored between her legs. Wondered what she would do if she suddenly opened her eyes and saw him gazing upon her nakedness.

But she was a heavy sleeper. A woman who enjoyed sleeping in the nude, occasionally kicking off her blankets and giving him one hell of an eyeful of her beautiful body.

Jacob's shaft hardened at the memory.

The movement of his erection against the blanket covering him caught his attention. His gaze traveled over his healthy bulge, and he found himself looking toward the foot of the bed.

Two feet of space separated the bed from the south wall and the large octagonal window. Frilly yellow curtains hung at the sides of the half open window allowing sunshine and warm salty air to spill inside.

To add charm to the rustic white painted room, a bouquet of fresh looking yellow buttercups had been stuffed into a dented tin teapot set on the nearby wooden crate.

The roar of the pounding ocean surf drifted into the open window. It barely drowned out the squeaky sound from the rusty windmill perched on the nearby hill.

Other than that, silence permeated the air. It created a bad feeling inside Jacob.

Where was Hannah? Had she left him here? Abandoned him? Taken his father's stolen car? Made a mad dash for the border on her own?

He frowned. He hoped she hadn't run again. If his father had discovered the car she'd taken from the barn, she wouldn't have a chance. She'd be caught. The men at Border Patrol would take her into a backroom, do with her whatever they wanted to, and then simply kill her. Or if she wasn't lucky, they'd sell her on the black market as a Breeder Slave.

Jacob shuddered at that thought. He'd heard stories about the runaway Breeder Slaves who were unfortunate enough to get sold onto the black-market. Those slaves didn't get access to medical supplies during birthing or given the sexual disease shots all legal breeder slaves were required to get.

He clenched his jaws in frustration. He wished he knew where she was. He wished he could climb out of bed and go looking for her.

But he was so weary. Tired from the loss of blood. Heck he couldn't even lift his hand to scratch the odd little itch on his nose.

Shit! He hated feeling so useless.

He tensed at the hollow sound of an approaching car engine and reached for the gun he kept in his shoulder holster.

Panic gripped him when he realized he wasn't wearing it.

Or any clothes!

He was a sitting duck lying here. Defenseless. Totally useless.

His frantic gaze searched the room, and he spotted his gun and holster hanging on a peg just inside the open doorway.

He tried to shift his body, tried to get out of bed, but he couldn't move a damn muscle.

He heard the car door slam. And then a moment later a second door slammed.

His stomach sank.

There were two of them.

Had they followed Hannah here? Had she left his Hit car outside in plain sight? If she had, the tracking device would lead them directly to the mansion.

No, he'd already warned her about the device. She was smarter than that. She wouldn't put herself in such danger.

His blood ran cold in his veins at the next thought. Maybe she'd been caught and turned him in so she could get a better deal. She was so damned innocent. She could spill her guts all over the place, and they wouldn't treat her any better.

She was a Breeder Slave, for god's sake. She had no rights. Didn't she understand that?

Jacob swallowed the tight knot of fear as he heard someone stomp onto the back porch of the mansion two floors down. His heart picked up speed as he heard one set of footsteps climb up the stairs toward the attic.

Toward him!

He'd heard two car doors slam. Was the other person waiting outside?

A floorboard creaked near the top of the stairs.

The urge to lift the blankets over his head and lie as stiff as a corpse was so great he wished he could do it, but his arms were like lead weights.

A flicker of movement in the doorway made the breath in his lungs tighten painfully.

Suddenly, someone stuck their head inside, and Jacob just about shit.

"Hannah," he said softly.

Hannah smiled and walked into the room.

"Glad to see you're awake."

"Where the hell where you?"

"Sweet greetings to you, too." She smiled cheerfully and placed a cool hand on his forehead.

A whiff of her sexy fresh scent drifted into his nostrils, making him very aware of her.

"Where have you been, Hannah?"

"Grocery shopping."

"Are you crazy? You've compromised this place."

She frowned. "No one followed me."

"Now you're suddenly an expert on being followed? You didn't even see me watching you for two weeks."

A teasing glint ripped through her eyes, and she asked softly,

"Did you like what you saw?"

"I wouldn't be here lying in your bed if I didn't, Hannah," he whispered.

He didn't miss the visible tremor of anticipation zip through her body at his words.

She swallowed and said cheerfully, "Well, obviously you're on the mend. You're fever is gone and..." Before he could stop her, she lifted the blanket covering his wounded thigh. Tucking the softness of the cloth close to his suddenly semi-aroused shaft, she thankfully draped his erection, keeping it hidden from her view. He had no doubt her eyes would widen with surprise if she saw the full extent of how much he truly desired her.

Cool air drifted against his thigh as she slowly peeled away the white patch covering his bullet wound.

"I must admit I make a pretty good doctor, don't you think?" she asked as she probed gently around the ragged edges of the hole.

"A pretty sexy doctor," he found himself muttering.

"Definitely on the mend," she chirped sweetly.

And then he remembered that she wasn't alone.

"Who's with you?"

"No one."

"I heard two car doors slam."

"Mercy! Aren't you the paranoid one? I had groceries in the back seat."

"You didn't use my car, did you? I told you...."

"It's at the bottom of the ocean about twenty miles up the coast. I took care of the tracking device before giving it the final farewell."

"Thank God," he sighed.

"I'm a little more resourceful than you seem to think I am. I towed your car using my car ... I mean your father's car…and sent yours over the cliff. Then I went to town and bought some groceries."

"Anyone recognize you?"

"Would I be here if they had?" she said as she reached for an antique bottle containing some yellowy liquid set on the nearby crate. She squeezed the gooey fluid onto a fresh bandage.

"I put on a wig that I found in an old chest in the basement. Wore a pair of sunglasses and acted natural. No one gave me a second look."

"I'm sure the men noticed you," Jacob mumbled.

She winked at him. "I don't think men would be interested in a gray haired old woman wearing black clothing and hobbling around with a cane."

"I'd recognize you wearing anything…or nothing."

"Well obviously you are in no position to find out how I look wearing anything," she teased.

Jacob inhaled as she placed the cool ointment riddled bandage onto his burning thigh. He shouldn't have done that, inhaled that is.

He could smell her again. A delicate scent of perfumed soap. It made him remember the mornings he'd watched her bathe in the ocean. The familiar need, sharp and deep wrenched through his shaft, hardening him even more.

"Sorry. I didn't mean to hurt you."

"You could never hurt me, Hannah." Unless he lost her.

"I'm glad to hear that because this might be a little uncomfortable." She ripped off some tape strips from a tape roll and pressed them tightly over the bandage and onto his flesh.

He couldn't stop himself from wincing at the tender pain around his wound or prevent his body from reacting to her deliciously fresh scent.

Boy! If he weren't so damn weak, he'd be taking her into his arms right now.

"There. How does that feel?"

"As long as you keep your hand there, it'll feel good."

To his surprise, she did keep her fingers pressed gently against his flesh. She peered curiously at him.

"Why did you put your life in jeopardy by telling the other Hitman you were letting me go?"

Jacob shrugged.

Hannah sighed in frustration and shook her head.

"Your picture is plastered all over the newspapers y'know.

"Already?"

"We've been here for three days, Jacob."

"What?"

"You had a bad fever, and I didn't know if..." Her eyes closed, and she visibly shuddered.

"You care if I die?"

Her eyes popped open. The sight of tears glistening in her green eyes stunned him.

"You saved my life. I owe you."

Of course. He understood now. She had only saved his life because he'd saved hers back at the hotel. She felt nothing but gratitude toward him. He'd been stupid to think otherwise.

"I guess we're even then," Jacob said dully.

She nodded and pulled her hand off his thigh.

"I'll go make you something to eat. It'll give you strength. Before you know it you'll be out of bed."

"I'd rather stay in bed ... with you."

She laughed. "You're definitely on the mend, Jacob. But you'll have to get out of bed in order to catch me."

Having said that, Hannah danced out the doorway blowing him kisses as she went.

"You better make it a good meal, Hannah!" he called to her retreating figure, "Because when I catch you I won't be letting you go."

"Promises. Promises."

Jacob's heart melted at the sound of her laughter as she descended the stairs.

Cripes!

She was going to make him explode with want. He'd better hurry up and get better because if the steely hardness of his aching shaft was any indication, he'd be needing it to change her attitude from laughter into excruciating cries of pure passion.

Chapter Five

It was late that evening when Hannah decided she would look in on Jacob one more time before turning in for the night. A good thing too because she caught him red-handed trying to wiggle his way out of bed.

"Oh, no you don't!" she shouted as she rushed over and pushed him back down against the pillows. "Do you want to reopen that bullet wound?"

"I need to get out of bed, Hannah. All this lying around is killing me." He sighed heavily and plopped his head back against the headboard with a dull thud.

"You can't get up until at least tomorrow morning. Until then, you're my prisoner, and you'll do as I say."

His frown turned into a teasing grin.

"Your prisoner? I like the thought of you doing whatever you want to me."

Hannah couldn't stop the warmth from cascading into her cheeks.

"By the way your face is flushing I think you like the idea, too."

She knew she should say something or at the very least deny that the thought of him being at her mercy excited her. For the life of her she couldn't acknowledge it out loud. If she did, she'd have to admit to herself she had sincere sexual feelings for him, too. The next natural step would be to give him her body and ultimately her heart.

And she wasn't prepared to do that.

She wanted her freedom, and she couldn't have it with Jacob.

Or could she?

Was there a possibility they could be together? He was now on the run, like she was. Both had hits on their heads. Both needed to get out of the country.

Oh God, dare she hope that they could have a future together?

"Hello? Hannah?"

Startled out of her daydream, Hannah looked up to find him staring right into her eyes.

"I didn't mean to embarrass you," he said softly.

"You didn't. I only want what's best for you. And right now that means you staying in bed."

Hannah swallowed tightly as he studied her. That gentleness she remembered from years ago was now reflected in his blue eyes. It gave her a warm feeling. A feeling she really liked.

"What's best for me is to get out of this bed and get you somewhere safe."

Once again he struggled to get into a seated position.

Despair ripped through her. It was too early for him to get out of bed. What she needed was a distraction.

"Wait! How about I give you a massage?"

That did the trick. He stopped struggling.

The pout he'd been favoring vanished. The corners of his sensual mouth lifted into a sexy grin.

Her heart fluttered.

Did he remember? Did he remember how she'd poured the yarrow healing oil onto various parts of his body while he'd slept? Did he remember how in his delirious state he'd reacted to her touch?

"A massage does sound appetizing."

Hannah detected the lust in his voice. Her nerve endings zipped with excitement. The thought of touching Jacob's flesh while he was fully awake and aware made her breath back up in her lungs.

"Unless you're afraid of me?"

Oh but she was. Afraid of how her body reacted every time she looked at him. Afraid of the way her breasts swelled and throbbed with the need of his touch every time his eyes brushed across them. Afraid of the way her cunt muscles quivered with a hungry ache when she envisioned how his thickness would stretch her vaginal muscles as he plunged inside her.

"I'm not afraid of you," she found herself whispering.

"Then let's get down to business." He rubbed his hands together in anticipation. "You can start on my legs. They need a good rub down."

To her surprise, he stuck out a very large, very bare foot from under the covers and wiggled his long toes at her.

"Don't you think my toes are cute?"

Hannah laughed, some of the tension easing away from her.

With suddenly trembling fingers, she lifted the bottle containing her yarrow healing oil from the crate where she kept it beside the vase of buttercups she'd picked early this morning.

She walked to the foot of his bed.

Jacob's fierce gaze followed her every move as she pulled away the blankets, revealing his long muscular legs. Bunching the covers just above the bullet wound, she held her breath and gazed at the leg muscles she'd become intimate with while she'd kept him drugged with her herbal teas. Drugged in an effort to allow his wound to heal. Or maybe she'd kept him doped up because she wasn't yet prepared to allow his promise of making her his own come true?

"They're only legs. They won't bite you," he teased.

The man was maddening. Didn't he know how lethal his legs really were?

She could still remember the silky heat of his muscular thighs as he'd straddled each side of her hips intimately when they'd fallen on the beach after he'd chased her.

Mercy it suddenly seemed warm in here.

"Why don't you sit between my legs?"

Hannah blinked at his boldness. "What?"''

"Sit between my legs. It'll be easier for you to have access to whatever you want ... or need."

Was that humor in his voice? Was that dangerous desire glittering in those dark green eyes?

"It's only a massage," he teased.

Of course it was only a massage. What in the world had she been thinking? Silly thoughts, that's what.

The man was as weak as a babe for heaven's sake. All she was doing was trying to distract him for a while with an innocent massage.

Despite telling herself this was all innocent, Hannah's mouth suddenly seemed too dry as she climbed onto the bed and sat cross-legged between his widespread legs.

Avoiding his intense gaze, she poured some oil into the palm of her hand.

She began working on his luscious toes, massaging one strong member after another, and then she graduated to one extremely large foot and then the other.

"Hannah, you are heaven sent." His eyes fluttered closed.

Hannah's oil slicked fingers slid easily over his hot skin and sunk deep into the bands of firm muscles lining his calves. She caressed his kneecaps and massaged the tight knots riddling his lower thighs.

Jacob said nothing. His eyes stayed shut, his body in a seemingly relaxed state.

Good.

Relaxed was just the way she needed him. It would keep his teasing words at bay and his sexy gaze from unraveling her.

When she neared the bandaged area on his upper thigh, he flinched, and she backed off.

"Please, don't stop," he groaned.

"But it hurts."

"Nothing I can't handle." A sweet smile lifted his sensuous lips.

Slowly Hannah peeled away the tape covering the wound. "Looks good. No sign of infection. It's healing nicely."

She poured more healing oil onto her palm and began massaging the surrounding tender muscles, smiling at the way the tips of his lips grimaced.

She inched higher and suddenly stopped when she realized the blankets had somehow moved up in such a way that his massive arousal partially peeked out at her.

Hannah gulped at the pleasing sight.

Heavens! No wonder he'd been quiet. He'd been thoroughly enjoying her touch!

"Hannah." She heard the tortured need for release in his voice.

She looked up to see his gaze centered on her mouth, his blue eyes dark with savage lust. The seductive look made her body burn with fire. Made her breathing go ragged. Her heart pound with anticipation.

She almost cried out at the shivers of excitement ripping through her limbs when he lifted the blanket, giving her full view of his unbelievably thick shaft. If she thought he was monstrous while she'd explored his body as he'd lain helpless in a delirious state, he was massive now.

Her pulses pounded, and her mouth watered at the delicious site. His thick bulging shaft stood straight up like a steel rod, the thick head purple with want.

It was a seductive invitation. One she couldn't refuse.

"I'll have to be very careful not to reopen the wound when I massage there." She hadn't realized she'd spoken aloud. The pleasing smile on his face told her she had.

Eagerness roared through her body, and she poured more oil onto her palms. Lowering her hands over his unbelievably tight testicles, he groaned as she squeezed gently.

"Breathe deeply," she whispered, saying it more to herself than to him.

She began to massage his hot flesh. His cock grew visibly harder. Veins pulsed on both sides of his shaft. The head bulged and begged for her attention, but Hannah avoided the area in question. There were other areas to attend to before coming to rest on her big prize.

Her hands left his testicles. She smoothed her fingers over his pubic bone, rubbing and kneading until his breathing deepened and grew hoarse.

Maintaining eye contact with him, she poured a small quantity of oil onto his shaft. Placing her right hand at the base, Hannah squeezed gently, smiling at Jacob's low growl of approval.

Pulling up, she slid her hand off, immediately replacing her left hand at the base of his penis, doing the same. Pulling up and sliding off. Right hand. Left hand. Varying the pressure, she took her time and continued to whisper at him to breathe deeply.

Then Hannah changed her strategy.

Squeezing the thick head of his silk encased penis as if it were an orange and she were putting it through a fruit squeezer, she then slid her right hand down his entire shaft and off, alternating left and right.

"You do it better than any other woman, Hannah," he murmured.

A wave of jealousy zipped through her when she remembered Jacob had been with many other women and she was probably just another notch in his belt.

What she wouldn't do to try and find out his true feelings about her.

An idea came swiftly to mind, and she couldn't help but smile inwardly. The Breeder Slaves knew of an ancient technique they sometimes used on males whom they had feelings for or on the males who seemed genuinely interested in the Slaves as a person and not just a cunt.

She'd never had the occasion to use the technique, but she remembered the instructions very well. If she did this right, she'd have Jacob revealing how he truly felt about her.

Trying hard not to get overly excited at what she was about to do, Hannah leisurely moved away from his aroused shaft and dipped a finger to the area below his once again tight testicles.

Kneading her finger gingerly along the perineum toward his anus she soon located what she was looking for.

"Breathe deep and slow while I tend to your Sacred Spot."

"Sacred Spot?" Confusion etched his husky voice.

"This area here," she said as she pressed against a tiny pea-shaped hollow halfway between his anus and his scrotum. "It may feel uncomfortable at first, but give me a little time, and I'll have you feeling very nice."

"I already feel very nice." He grinned, and his gaze traveled to his erect penis. Hannah savored the sensations that coursed through her cunt at the thought of how powerful his thrusts might be.

Gently she pressed against the slight indentation.

It felt hard. Tight. Tense.

Jacob squirmed against her delicate pressure, but Hannah didn't let go.

"How does it feel?" she asked.

"A pressure. Deep inside. It's uncomfortable like you said."

Hannah detected the anguish in his voice, the sparkles of pain in his blue eyes. Despite his distress, she kept on the pressure.

"My mother and the other Breeder Slaves used to whisper about this area on a man's body. The Sacred Spot stems from an ancient ritual, a lost science from our ancestors. By massaging the Sacred Spot, a man's body may be able to relax in a way he's never relaxed before, allowing certain emotions to come to the forefront, ultimately granting him great physical and emotional release. It's believed many ailments can be cured with this type of massage."

"No pain, no gain." A little frown worried his forehead.

He bit his lower lip as she increased the pressure, being especially careful not to press too hard on the sensitive spot.

"Another side effect is that after a man's Sacred Spot has been massaged, he will experience fantasy dreams for many nights."

He threw her a wobbly smile. "Bring on the fantasies."

"Why fantasize when you can have the real thing," she whispered.

His aroused inhalation gave her the encouragement she needed to ask more questions.

"The other day in the car just after you'd been shot, you promised you'd take me, Jacob. You promised you'd make me your own in every way a man makes a woman his. Was that the truth? Or am I just another notch in your belt?"

His eyes darkened dangerously, and desire curled through her body.

"I've always wanted you, Hannah. From the first time my father brought you home."

"Why? Is it a physical attraction? Or is it more?"

He blinked in surprise at her question.

"What you're asking is do I want to have a serious relationship with you after the sex is over?"

Hannah could feel her face flame with embarrassment. She half expected him to laugh. Expected him to remind her she had no rights. That she was a Breeder Slave and he was a rich Breeder Plantation owner's son. That she was having delusions of grandeur.

"I'm a killing machine, Hannah. Trained to follow orders. They trained me so damned good, I almost killed you the other day on the beach, despite my feelings for you. Even before I approached you, I had a rifle aimed at your heart. I had my finger on the trigger. I could have killed you."

"But you didn't."

"I almost did, and that's too close."

Beneath her finger, his Sacred Spot tensed up again. Obviously, he had plenty of anger brewing inside him. The same raw anger and frustration she possessed at being trapped in a life in which she had no say.

"We're victims, Jacob. Victims of an oppressive dictatorship society."

"I know all about being oppressed, Hannah. That's just the way it is. There's nothing we can do about it. But I know one thing for certain, I want you to be safe. Safe from the men who make the rules. Safe from me."

"Why should I be safe from you?"

Jacob's Adam's apple bobbed wildly as he swallowed.

That familiar look of fear clouded his eyes. It was the same fear she'd seen when she'd approached him in the meadow a few days ago.

Hannah's heart began to pound violently. "What are you afraid you'll do to me?"

"I'm sure you've heard the rumors from the other Breeder Slaves."

Hannah shivered with excitement.

"Are those rumors true?"

"Yes."

Hannah's pulse roared.

"If I weren't as weak as I am right now, I'd be pounding into you without mercy, Hannah. Thrusting myself into you for hours, and you'd be begging me to never stop, just like the other Breeder Slaves did."

Heat burned through her body at his sensual admission. Heat and an insane thrill to experience what he was telling her made moisture grow between her legs.

His hand reached down, grabbed her wrist, and roughly pulled her finger away from his hot Sacred Spot. His blue eyes impaled her, preventing her from looking away.

"You've got the answers to what you've been looking for, Hannah. I think it's time you leave my Sacred Spot alone and concentrate on something else. Like saving your energy for the things I've got planned for you."

The threat in his words made her ache to have his arms around her. Made her want his hands to touch her, to roam all over her body. To touch every part of her being.

And she wanted to touch him. To make him see she wasn't afraid of what he wanted to do to her.

"Lucky for you, I don't scare easily. Lucky for me, you're at my mercy," she whispered.

Without warning, Hannah bent over and licked the pulsing head of his giant cock. He was so deliciously hard against her soft tongue. So hard and so hot. She liked the taste of him. The taste of man. The taste of masculine sex.

He groaned.

The wild sound fueled the desire already engulfing her body. Suddenly she wanted to feel his flesh pulse against her lips. Wanted to feel the power of his masculine hardness.

Opening her mouth wide, she slid the head of his cock past her lips. His flesh burned fiercely and throbbed violently against her hungry tongue. She liked the velvety feel of his penis, loved the feel of the solid muscle, the power that pulsed inside her mouth.

She liked it a lot.

From the corner of her eye she noticed his gaze darken with lust. The darkest she'd ever seen them.

In response, she tightened her lips around his cock, her tongue meeting his bulging tip, mating with it, making him groan again.

She took more of him into her mouth, her lips caressed his hard powerful length. Her tongue stroked and slurped his organ, and when the tip of his hot flesh touched the back of her throat, Hannah stopped.

Dangerous desire ripped through her like a roaring fire.

Now was her chance to would prove to him that she wasn't afraid of those rumors. Rumors of how he could thrust into a Breeder Slave's mouth for hours on end without spilling his seed.

Deep in her heart she knew that if all those rumors were true, she'd love whatever he did to her.

* * * *

Jacob tried to hold back the groans, but he couldn't do it. Hannah was an expert with her lips. She'd been trained well by his father. Trained to pleasure a man in ways that would have him aching for relief within minutes.

But he'd trained himself, too.

Trained himself to experience multiple orgasms without ejaculating. He'd had plenty of opportunities over the years. One of his jobs at his father's Breeding Plantation had been to fuck the Breeder Slaves who'd just reached Breeder Slave status. That's what the Breeding Ceremonies had been designed for. To introduce the woman to her new life. Since the Breeder Slave had the right to keep her first-born, it wasn't important who the father of her first child would be. What was important was to get the slave pregnant as fast as possible so the first baby would be born freeing up the Slave to produce further children for the many desperate and rich couples who yearned for one.

The Breeding Slave was also put into the Breeding Catalog. Couples would pick out which two Breeder Slaves they wanted to produce a child for them.

The Slaves would be paired and kept in a Breeding Pen until the female was pregnant. Sometimes the couples watched the Breeder Slaves they'd picked. Watched to see how their child was conceived.

Jacob had always thought this was a normal part of life. Hadn't thought anything unnatural about the endless fucking parties with the new female Breeder Slaves. Hadn't thought anything was wrong by forcing women to pop out numerous children as if they were on some assembly line.

Things had changed when he'd gone to Hit School and met Tool.

Tool, who had been his roommate and somewhat of a history buff. He'd whispered about illegal things. Like the days when all women and men had been free to choose what jobs and partners they wanted. He'd been the one who had encouraged Jacob to work for the affections of a free female and not just go off and satisfy himself with a Breeder Slave whenever the urge hit.

Tool had encouraged him to pursue Hitgals at the school. And Jacob had. He'd tried to woo them like Tool had taught him. By going out on dates. Taking them to dinner, the movies, coffee. But every time he'd go out on a date with one of them, he'd felt guilty at enjoying the woman's company, and his thoughts would ultimately turn to Hannah.

Lovely Hannah with the silky black hair, gorgeous green eyes, and a succulent mouth that was working wonders on his throbbing erection.

He watched her work on him. Watched the lust twinkling in her eyes as her hot, moist lips clamped over his hard cock. Her mouth stretched open wide as she welcomed his massive length inside. He watched as she hollowed out her cheeks and gave him some extra strong sucks.

Blades of sharp lightning seared along the length of his throbbing shaft and rammed straight into his balls, tightening them into painful knots of need and urging him to ejaculate into her seductive mouth.

Gathering all his self-control, he fought frantically to not give into his release. He wanted this pleasure to last. He wanted her to make love to his throbbing cock with her succulent lips. Most of all he wanted to be healthy and fit so he could fuck her for days on end until she begged him to stop the delicious torture.

But for now, he'd take her anyway he could get her. And she was doing a damn fine job with his cock.

Hunger flooded her features, and she sucked harder, making him gasp at her desperation. Before long, his hips were thrusting upwards into her mouth, begging her to bring him to release.

But he wouldn't give in so easily. He'd make her work for a taste of him.

As if sensing he was holding himself back, she sucked harder. Delicious orgasms rippled through his cock, and he shuddered beneath her beautiful mouth's onslaught.

Still he refused to come. Refused to give up this excruciating satisfaction of having the woman he'd always wanted actually making love to his cock with her mouth.

She kept up the onslaught. He rode the oncoming orgasms ripping through his body. Rode them with all his might until he hovered at the brink of insanity.

Finally he could take the agonizing pleasure no longer and dragged his hands through her silky hair, clasped her head still, and, holding her steady, he began to thrust in and out of her mouth.

Warning her he was going to come soon, he was surprised to find the sucking on his dick increase into a wild frenzy of want.

Damn! Did the woman ever tire?

She sucked harder until she totally destroyed his self-composure, his body tightened, the pleasure too overwhelming.

Finally he gave into the pressure and released his hot load.

The long column of her graceful neck convulsed as she greedily swallowed his love seed. Tiny sexy whimpers filled the air as she kept sucking, kept draining him. Eventually, he sighed as immense relief swept his body when she finally sucked him dry.

He let go of her head and leaned back against the headboard, totally spent and wholly satisfied.

He'd been right about Hannah. She was the only woman for him. The only woman who could shatter his self control so quickly. The only woman who could spear through the lust he'd harbored inside him and satisfy his needs.

Best of all she was the only woman who could bring back the man he'd once been.

The only way he could think to thank her was to return the favor.

Chapter Six

Hannah laid her head on Jacob's firm stomach and listened to his shaky breathing.

She shouldn't have been so rough on him. Shouldn't have taken advantage of his weakness. But the power pulsing through his shaft had challenged her to break that steel hardness. And she'd been well rewarded for her efforts because his come had tasted absolutely delicious.

A perfect combination of salt and spice. She couldn't wait to taste him again.

Her body hummed with desire. She wanted him badly. But he needed his rest. He needed to recuperate.

"Where is it?" he suddenly asked.

"What?"

"Your dildo."

She blinked in shock.

"I know you have it. I saw you using it many times over those two weeks when you thought you were alone up here in this room..." His words faded away.

Hannah couldn't believe her own excitement at the thought that he'd watched her masturbate.

"Get it," he ordered.

She found herself nodding.

On trembling legs, Hannah retrieved the giant rubber dildo with balls from where she'd stashed it in its handy container in the tiny attic closet. Mere days ago she'd left it here with a heavy heart, sure she would never see it again. The risk of it being found on her had been too high. And the punishment for possessing such a toy was severe.

A strange little smile flittered across his face as he examined it closely.

"Almost as big as me." He cocked a curious eyebrow at her. "Breeder Slaves aren't allowed to have sex toys. Where'd you get it?"

Hannah felt her spine bristle in sudden anger.

"I'm not a slave anymore, Jacob. The sooner you get used to that idea, the better."

He ignored her comment and continued to examine the massive dildo.

"Take off your pants and underwear, Hannah. I'm going to punish you for holding illegal toys."

Despite the fact he was ordering her with the firm tone of voice men reserved for Breeder Slaves, Hannah felt strangely thrilled at the idea of having to stand totally naked in front of Jacob. And at having him dish out the punishment.

Her heart pounded with excitement as she slowly tugged off her shorts and slid her underwear down her legs.

She stepped out of them and lifted her head to find Jacob's eyes sparkling with desire, his gaze focused between her thighs. The tip of his pink tongue poked through his seductive lips.

She remembered his strong tongue slamming into her wet cunt as she'd lain on the sandy beach, her legs stretched wide open for him, the succulent pleasures ripping apart her body as he'd sipped her wetness.

"Take off your top," he demanded.

She didn't miss the way his fingers tightened around her dildo. Didn't miss the heated look burning in his dark blue eyes as he watched her. Or the increasing sound of his raspy breathing.

With her breath hitched in her lungs, she peeled off her tank top, allowing her heavy breasts to bounce free into the cool night air.

Jacob hissed sharply between his teeth.

"Come here." The demand was no more than an aroused whisper.

He patted his bare stomach. "Settle your ass here and face me."

"I can't sit on you. You're injured."

"My leg is injured. The rest of me is quite healthy, as you've experienced. Besides you aren't that heavy. Now come. Sit here."

Sweet mercy! What was he planning to do to her?

Her heart crashed violently against her chest, and a tinge of fear ripped up her spine, but she did as he commanded.

Climbing over him, she nestled her butt onto his muscular belly, facing him. Heat seared through her ass, and she tried hard to ignore the blossoming hard-on pressed against her backside.

"Keep your hands to your sides while I look at you."

She did as he ordered. Letting her arms dangle at her sides. Her hands knotted into frustrated fists, and she struggled against the need to run her fingers through the sparse thatch of his crisp chest hairs.

Placing her dildo on a nearby pillow, he reached out and

intimately palmed her breasts in his hot wide hands.

"You are so beautiful, Hannah," he whispered as he gazed into her eyes. His thumbs softly caressed her nipples, releasing carnal sparks of electricity. Within seconds she found herself whimpering with need.

"I've wanted to touch you for years. I've wanted to fuck you since the first minute I saw you."

"Why didn't you?" Arching her back, she pressed her sensitive breasts against his probing fingers.

"You know why."

"No, I don't. Tell me."

Jacob inhaled a shuddering breath, and he frowned. His fingers thankfully kept plumping her now sensitized nipples with firm pinches.

"My father said it would be a scandal if I took you for my own."

Hannah blinked in surprise.

"You told your father you were interested in me?"

"I told him. Now, lean back. Spread your legs."

Quickly, she did as he said.

His long fingers slid against her clit, and he began rubbing her pleasure nub, producing incredible sensations she'd never experienced before. Moisture quickly accumulated between her legs, and she knew he was readying her for her punishment at being caught with a sex toy.

"I told him I wanted you as my wife," he continued softly.

"Your wife?" Dare she hope he was telling the truth?

"Yes."

Her body trembled with excitement at his admission.

"But you never so much as touched me. Never gave me an inkling of how you truly felt, except for being nice to me."

"Believe me, I wanted you. I just didn't know how to tell you."

"But you had the courage to tell your father?"

"Yes, I told him."

"I bet your father wasn't pleased."

"He sent me to Hit School the very next day."

A mixture of anger and relief spilled through Hannah. Relief because she'd always wondered why he hadn't said goodbye. Anger because his father had come between them.

Jacob's head lowered, and she gasped as he took a nipple into his moist mouth. Suckling sounds rent the night air. And the probing of his hot tongue and nipping of his sharp teeth produced delightful sensations within her breast along with an aching fullness she'd never experienced before.

"I'm glad you finally came home," she whispered and arched her back, pushing her breast tighter into his hot face.

His suckling stopped.

Hannah sighed with frustration as he lifted his head.

"I came back for you, Hannah. I came back with full intentions of being the first and only Romero brother to fuck you in the Breeding Stall. I wanted to impregnate you with my seed. I wanted your first child to be mine. To be ours. I wanted everyone to know you were mine. The night before I left for Hit School, I warned my brother's not to touch you, Hannah. I told them you were mine."

"Your warning worked. They never touched me. They didn't even look at me," she said softly.

"If they had, I would have killed them." His voice was too calm and too deadly.

A shiver of fear zipped up her spine at the thought that Jacob had threatened death to his very own brothers because of her.

The fear, however, was quickly extinguished when his sensual lips clamped around her nipple again.

The long hot fingers quickened at her clit. Moving in erotic circles until hot pleasure spilled through her insides. Within seconds, she was arching her hips upward.

She closed her eyes, physically tightening her cunt muscles, fully intent on making herself climax.

"Keep your eyes open, Hannah. This is your punishment for harboring a sex toy. I want to watch you suffer."

Her eyes flew open and locked onto his piercing gaze. Incredible sensations slammed through her body at the mixture of emotions flooding his eyes.

There was tenderness.

Lust.

Excitement.

Caring.

"Spread your legs wider and lean back against my legs so I can get a good look at that beautiful cunt of yours."

She leaned backwards until her back settled against his powerful thighs. He'd lifted his knees in an effort to support her. And he hadn't so much as flinched at moving his wounded thigh.

He would be healthy very soon. Healthy and full of power, his body ready to unleash a ravenous hunger for a woman.

Her heart beat violently against her chest at that thought and at the sight of his fierce gaze clamping onto her cunt. She could almost feel his eyes caress her clit as he stared.

"Tomorrow I'm going to take you. Make you my woman. Tonight though," He lifted her giant sex toy off the nearby pillow, and she felt it nudge into her moist opening. "Tonight, I'll show you what it feels like to have a man masturbate you."

He pushed the dildo into her slowly, her vaginal muscles gripping the item hungrily, her hips arching eagerly toward him, wanting him to go faster. Wanting him to bring about a quick release.

Unfortunately, Jacob had other things on his mind.

She moaned when his fingers touched her left nipple. He twisted the quivering bud until she gasped out at the sliver of pain. And then his fingers attacked her other one, twisting until he heard her cry out.

At the same time, he was sinking the dildo deep into her body. Her inner muscles gripped it madly in an effort to suck it in. Yet he continued to go so erotically slow that Hannah screamed out her frustration.

"I warned you, Hannah. I warned you that you weren't safe with me. I warned you...."

Pleasant sensations ran along her cunt, and Hannah closed her eyes.

"Keep looking at me, Hannah." His command was sharp, making her eyes snap open.

Through heavy lids she watched the hungry look crawl into Jacob's eyes as he watched her. Out of nowhere a mind-shattering climax took her by surprise, exploding through her body with such a wild intensity she screamed out his name.

Another explosion came, followed by more. The intensity of them made her cry out, made her mind splinter as they carried her away.

His thrusts grew more forceful, the climaxes slammed into her in killing waves of pleasure that left her gasping for her breath over and over again.

She grabbed his hips for support, her fingers digging into his muscles.

Heavens! He was destroying her with her own dildo. Fire lanced through her cunt as a calloused thumb grated across the bundle of nerves between her legs.

"You like what I'm doing to you, Hannah?" he whispered hotly.

Hannah couldn't speak. She was too busy concentrating on the heated pleasure spreading like wildfire through her body.

Her breasts heaved frantically as the orgasms continued to race through her. His plunging strokes expertly hit sensitive points on the way in. And on the way out he grated along nerve endings she'd never known existed.

She was lost in a mind storm of incredible sensations she'd never experienced before. Lost in the burning lust he'd unleashed inside her. Lost in the hot need for release.

Her hips gyrated beneath the onslaught. The suctioning sound of the dildo sliding in and out of her flew into the air, intermingling with her gasps of joy.

He thrust harder. She moaned. Arched her back. Ached for more of this insanity. Frantically, she pressed against the fraying thumb that circled her slippery clit in a whirlwind of pressure.

Perspiration broke out all over her body as one climax after another shattered her mind and tortured her body.

The dildo continued to impale her, and she finally came violently in a shuddering rush.

"Yes! That's it! Come for me, my sweet Hannah. Come for me."

Hot juice slid from her body along with the dildo. Suddenly, his hot hands clasped her ass tightly. He lifted her hips upward, and his head sank between her legs. His burning lips suckled her clit, and he sipped greedily of her hot liquid gift, sending her headlong into another wild climax.

* * * *

Hannah lay quiet on his torso, her body truly spent. Her breaths came in sweet little gasps, her legs still quivered and were spread wide when Jacob lifted his head and smiled at her sleeping form.

Her eyes were closed tightly as she slept. A sweet smile tilted her ruby red lips. Her breasts were still swollen with desire, her large nipples rouge from his painful ministrations.

"You did a fine job, Hannah. A fine job," he said softly, careful not to arouse her from her sleep.

The sweet taste of her come was hot in his mouth. It made him think of the way her face had scrunched up in ecstasy as he'd slammed the dildo into her. Made him remember the lovely way her breasts had swelled with pleasure and heaved wildly under her labored breaths while he'd touched her silky flesh.

He loved the way her hips had gyrated with convulsions. He'd become addicted to the site of her purple swollen clit, the incredible sight of the large dildo disappearing into her tight hole, and the way it slurped out again drenched in her cunt juices.

The sight had made him hornier than hell.

Made him imagine sinking into her, stretching into her warmth. Made him imagine how her cunt muscles would wrap around his rod as his thick intrusion forced its way home.

But all that would wait until tomorrow.

For now they would rest.

Gently, he lifted her sleeping form and positioned her beside him. He drew the warm blankets over their nude bodies and found himself smiling.

"This was just the beginning, Hannah. Just the beginning. Tomorrow I will make you mine."

* * * *

Pink and gold rays of dawn spilled over Jacob as he lay quietly in the bed. His body, however, was anything but quiet. As a matter of fact, it was humming. And he was hornier than hell.

Clenching his fists in frustration, he closed his eyes and remembered last night.

Remembered the way her silky fingers had rubbed his flesh.

He'd memorized the sweet scent of her clit. The sexy taste of her tight nipples in his mouth. The seductive sounds of her soft whimpers as he'd plunged the massive dildo into her juicy cunt.

God, he wanted Hannah more now than he'd ever wanted her. What had she done to him last night? Why had she asked all those curious questions? Why had he answered?

Last night her sensual touches had freed his emotions. Brought out the anger, the frustrations he'd stored inside him. Her touch had given him a glimpse of freedom, and it had tasted fabulous.

Addictive.

Addictive like Hannah. Last night he hadn't been able to get enough of touching her, of tasting her.

He wanted more.

So much more.

Sharp pain radiated through his thigh as he climbed out of bed, but he could stand it.

What he couldn't stand was being away from Hannah.

The time had finally come to show her how much he wanted her.

* * * *

Hannah dipped a toe into the ocean waters and smiled. Perfect temperature for an early morning bath. Within seconds, she was naked, a bar of soap in her hand and up to her waist in the crashing surf.

The water relaxed her as it cradled her body with its soothing salty liquid. Using the soap, she lathered her dark tresses and at the same time kept a careful watch on the brightening silhouette of the mansion perched nearby.

Erosion from the ocean had brought the beach practically up to its back door. The giant stone building looked magnificent as the dawn colors of pink and gold splashed against the cracked and dusty windows.

It would be such a beautiful place to live in. No one would have to know they were here. They wouldn't even have to go to town for food. The surrounding buttercup riddled fields could be ploughed. They could plant enough vegetables to get them through a winter.

The area was teaming with rabbits for meat. And they could fish in the ocean. Fruit could come from the numerous apple and pear trees she'd spotted in a nearby grove.

Hannah smiled and hugged herself.

They could have their own children. Children who were free. Children who could run along the beach, their faces flushed from excitement and tanned from the warm sunshine. Jacob and she could show them how to build sand castles, play games, and teach them as well as her how to read and write.

But before all that, she would ask Jacob to build a small boat, and they could sail into the sunset then come home and make love all night long.

And boy did he ever know how to make love with a dildo.

She could only imagine how it would be with the real thing buried deep inside her.

She shivered at the prospect. She needed to hurry. Needed to get herself ready for Jacob.

Splashing the water onto her head, she rinsed her hair, the anticipation growing inside her at the thought of finally experiencing all those delicious rumors she'd heard about Jacob.

"Good morning."

"Oh my goodness," she gasped as she spotted Jacob standing on the beach, barefoot and bare-chested wearing nothing but a pair of tattered green shorts she'd fashioned out of his uniform pants.

Suddenly unexplainably embarrassed, she instinctively turned her naked body away from him, showing him her bare back.

"No need for being shy anymore, Hannah. I've seen all of you. Why don't come on out of there so we can pick up where we left off last night? Or would you rather I come in?"

Hannah shivered with delight at his words and looked over her shoulder just in time to see him take a step forward.

"Don't! You'll get your bandage wet, Jacob."

"Then come on out, Hannah. I want to make love to you."

Was she dreaming? Was he actually saying he wanted to have sex with her again?

But why wouldn't he? He was a red-blooded male, and she knew they always wanted sex.

He took another step forward. Ocean waves crashed against his knees. Oh heavens, he wasn't ready for any acrobatic activities.

"Jacob, don't do anything foolish. You could re-injure yourself," she warned.

"I'll risk it. Turn around. Let me look at you."

Her heart thumped erratically at his demand. Turning slowly she allowed him to gaze upon her naked body.

Desire sparked his eyes, and she saw the bulge between his legs grow larger as it pressed against his tattered shorts.

Oh boy. The thought of his massive arousal sliding inside her took her breath away. Brought a wild thick heat surging through her blood.

Slowly, as if in a trance, Hannah kept her eyes glued to that lovely bulge as she moved through the waters toward him.

A moment later, his strong arms embraced her, his hot mouth melted fiery kisses all over her face, and then he whispered in her ear, "When I woke up and found you gone, I realized I never want to wake up without you again. The time has come for me to show you those rumors about me are true, Hannah."

At his words, she fought hard against the shivers of both fear and anticipation that roared through her body.

"I know you've wanted to see if those rumors are true." His head dipped down, and he kissed the valley between her breasts.

The intimate gesture weakened her, made her breasts heave with her every breath.

"I know you want me inside you, Hannah. I know you'd prefer me over your trusty dildo."

His hot mouth popped her right nipple into his mouth as if it were a ripe cherry. With his teeth he bit and nipped gently until pain and arousal pierced through her breast zipping all the way down into her cunt, making her wet with that now achingly familiar ferocious desire for him.

He released her now rock hard nipple and worked on the other one until her breast swelled with desire and she whimpered for relief.

His head lifted from his harsh nibbles on her breasts.

"Come, I've prepared a place for us."

Taking her by the hand, he led her out of the water across the warm sand into a nearby thicket.

Tall grass secluded them on three sides, allowing them only the full view of the white waves rolling upon the beach and the sparkling blue ocean waters.

In the thicket she spotted a large blanket laid out for them. Nestled in the tall grass she didn't miss a closed picnic basket.

"That's going to be our nourishment. We're going to need it because what I've planned for you will take a while." His lips caressed her neck with more tiny kisses. Kisses that made her heart flutter with joy.

"Jacob, are you sure you're up to this? I don't want you to re-injure yourself."

"After hearing your moans and whimpers last night while I made love to you with that dildo, you're damn right I'm up to this."

His hot hand slid across her waist and spanned over her belly, making her shiver with a brilliant need for him. A need for him to touch her everywhere.

"Show me those rumors, Jacob. Show me how much you want me." Her fingers curled around the waistband of his green shorts.

He inhaled sharply at her touch.

"I don't only want you, Hannah. I need to be inside you. I need to feel like a man again."

"And I need to feel like a woman. Fuck me, Jacob. Fuck me now. Take me without mercy. Show me how you make love to a woman."

Her fingers tore at his pants, yanking them down. His swollen shaft sprung free, and Hannah wasted no time wrapping her hands around his hot flesh.

She aimed his throbbing flesh toward her cunt, anxious for him to be inside her. Her body demanding to be taken. She brought the thickness of his pulsing rod to the door of her womanhood, and then she hesitated.

"There's something I need to tell you, Jacob. Something you need to know."

"You're picking one hell of a time to tell me, sweetie."

His hot lips nibbled on her earlobe, making Hannah's knees

weaken.

"You're my first real lover," she blurted out.

Shock and surprise flooded his dark eyes. "What?"

"Your father, he's the one who gave me the dildo so I could satisfy myself. He has an anal fetish, and your mother wouldn't allow him to, so he used me...."

A warm finger pressed gently against her lips, silencing her.

"Thank you for telling me, Hannah."

"You're not upset?"

He threw his head back as if in relief. A serene look flittered across his face, and he inhaled a shuddering breath.

"You don't know how happy this makes me. You don't know how long I've pictured my father and you together. It made me so angry. Made me want to kill him for taking you away from me."

"No man could ever change the attraction we have between us. Or the feelings I have for you."

To her surprise, his hand wrapped around her wrist holding his throbbing penis.

"What you've said changes things."

She cried out in protest as he guided her hand away from his thick penis.

His head bent closer, and his warm lips caressed the corners of her mouth until she sparkled with joy.

"I want your first time to be something you'll never forget."

His mouth moved over hers in a seductive manner, making her knees turn to jelly, making her body hum with raw desire. Instinctively, she knew once this man made love to her, she would belong to him.

Forever.

A warm hand settled over her stomach again. His finger delicately prodded at her belly button, immediately igniting a fire inside her womb that she'd never felt before. It was something so unbelievably beautiful she wondered if she would be able to stand the rest of what he had planned for her.

His finger explored her belly button with gentle circular motions, alternating between hard thrusts and delicate stabs similar to the way he'd drove the dildo into her cunt last night.

Dammed if this unfamiliar technique wasn't turning her on higher than a firecracker.

His hot mouth sucked at her lips until she opened them. Instantly, his tongue slid inside and clashed with her own, unleashing a firestorm of pleasure that had her whimpering into his mouth.

His probing finger withdrew from her belly button, and his hands covered her swelling breasts. Massaging her fullness, he shaped them with his palms, tweaking her nipples until they burned and ached beneath his caresses.

Before she knew what was happening, he lowered her to the warm blanket and onto her back.

He lay down beside her and curled her into his arms, spooning his heated body against her entire length, fitting his thick rod at the entrance of her cunt.

She inhaled with excitement at the hunger consuming his eyes. Inhaled his raw male scent and reveled in the strong odor of his lust.

"I'm going to start making love to you, Hannah. Don't be afraid. Just know you're safe with me."

She could barely nod, her body trembled with such a strong need to have him inside her.

His mouth quickly resumed kissing her, concentrating on the curves of her lip. He suckled her there. Suckled and nipped until her mouth was stoked with fire.

His thighs moved, and she felt his erection plow past her slippery labia lips as he entered her.

Pleasure centers she never knew had existed exploded to life as his tremendous size stretched vaginal muscles that had never been extended so wide. He hadn't entered two inches when her cunt muscles clamped around his thick rod throwing her instantly into a wild orgasm that left her body quaking and her hips shuddering.

When it was over, she realized Jacob was still sinking his length into her. Her cunt juices gushed around his thick rod, and her muscles quivered around him, welcoming him inside.

Surprisingly, she felt no pain at his invasion. Only an insane need to increase this erotic fullness. Arching her hips against him, she moaned as he sunk even deeper, and her vaginal muscles adjusted to the incoming slow moving missile.

The smell of her arousal intermingled with the salty air. The roar of ocean waves vanished as she listened to his increasingly harsh breathing. His hot chest flattened her breasts. His heart thumped wildly against her flesh. She could feel her own heart beat joining his in a foreplay of things to come.

Her body shuddered with fear as he flexed his hips. The movement plunged his thick rod deeper. He kept filling her and filling her.

She had never dreamed a man could fill her insides so much.

Another orgasm hit her, and Hannah's hips twisted wildly at the onslaught. She cried out at the intensity.

Fire screamed through every part of her body as his iron rod screamed past more pleasure centers.

She convulsed again and again. Finally his rod slammed into her womb, and she could feel his balls slap against her flesh as he finally came to the end.

"I'm glad to see my shaft has already pleasured you. And I haven't even started yet."

He grinned. His smile wicked with delicious promises. His gaze filled with lust as he looked deep into her eyes. Into her very soul.

"I'm going to brand your cunt with my cock, Hannah. I'm going to fuck you so much, no man will ever come close to satisfying you like I will. You will belong to me."

His words were spoken with such serious conviction she had no doubt he'd make sure she would never stray. It looked like she was about to experience another one of those Breeder Slaves rumors. Once a Slave had a Romero brother brand her cunt, the woman would never want any other man.

"Fuck me, Jacob." She grabbed at his shoulders, plunging her nails into the taut muscles in his back, pulling him closer.

Suddenly she was desperate. Desperate for him to do something. Anything to quench her desires.

Slowly he withdrew his massive rod and then speared back inside. She lost her breath at the ferocity of his power. Her fingernails dug deeper into his muscles, and she held on tight.

His plunging increased, and her cunt muscles convulsed around him.

Ripping his mouth free, he groaned into the air. His thrusts were measured. Deep. Hard. Creating such a firestorm inside her she soon hovered between two worlds.

Reality.

And a fantasy world sparkling with a dangerous pleasure so sharp and brilliant she found herself crying out at its intensity.

Her cunt muscles tightened harder around his cock. Squeezed him until his warm gasps caressed her cheeks

Hot perspiration popped onto her forehead, her face, and her entire body. Her cunt juices dripped from between her legs as he pounded into her. The sucking sound of it spurned him on with feverish, animalistic movements.

The scent of her sex hung heavy around them. It seemed to be an aphrodisiac for him. Seemed to make him thrust harder.

Suddenly, her mind shattered. Her body exploded into bliss and pain.

Yet he continued to ram into her.

She found herself screaming. Crying out as the fiery sensations rolled over her in excruciating waves.

She could barely catch her breath. Could barely hold onto her sanity. She was going to die from pleasure. She was going to die!

His animalist grunts continued. She followed the sounds. Tried to keep a lifeline to reality.

Another wild thrust, and she found the line yanked away. She fell into the other world. The world of blinding arousal, exhilarating pleasure, and an insane need to remain here for as long as she could.

Chapter Seven

They made love under the blanket of warm sunshine, stopping only to quench their thirst and to eat from the picnic basket nestled beside them.

When the cool canopy of dusk dropped over them, Jacob led Hannah inside the mansion where she was surprised to see a blanket draped a mattress lain out before the stone fireplace in the living room.

He'd planned everything so well.

From their love nest beside the beach, to the snug mattress in front of the fireplace, to the already set wood in the hearth.

All he did was light a match, and a friendly fire crackled, chasing away the chills of the oncoming September night. They lay on the mattress side by side staring into each other's eyes.

The intensity of his gaze made her heart leap with joy. Made her wonder how in the world she could ever live without Jacob. Or ever experience anything like she'd experienced today on the beach as he'd made love to her.

Without a doubt she was now a damaged Breeder Slave. Branded by this man's lust. Tied to him like she'd never been tied to anyone in her life.

"I think I need to check you wound," she said as she reached out and ran her hand along his bandaged thigh.

"I think I need to fuck you again."

"I like the sound of that. But first, I'll check the wound, Jacob."

"It's fine."

"I'll be the judge of that."

Before he could protest, she ripped the patch off his leg and examined the bullet hole.

"It looks a little bit red."

"I'm sure it'll be fine. Hardly hurts at all anymore. Come lay back down beside me. We'll rest and watch the fire for a little while."

Hannah nodded, excitement once again pounding through her nerve endings as she caught sight of his wonderful erection beginning to grow again. From the looks of it, this would be a very short rest.

Re-bandaging the wound, Hannah lay down on the soft mattress, and he curled her into his warm embrace.

"I'm glad you're here with me, Jacob."

"I'm glad I'm here with you, too. It's given me a break from reality. Given me time to explore my feelings and my fantasies about you." He inhaled a shuddering breath, and that dead look she detested suddenly flashed in his eyes. Her stomach clawed with sickness at the sight. He was about to tell her something she didn't want to hear.

"We're going to have to leave, Hannah. It won't be long before someone comes looking for us here."

Hannah sighed in relief and cuddled closer to his warmth.

"I should have told you this earlier, but we have to stay here," she whispered and traced a finger around a cute little laugh line at the side of his eye. "The Breeder Slaves said this a contact point with the Underground Railroad. They'll come for us. They'll take us to freedom."

"They're just rumors, Hannah."

"No, they aren't!" Sudden anger snapped inside her. "We're safe here as long as we keep out of sight. We can even stay here forever."

"We've been living on borrowed time, Hannah. I've decided we're going to leave first thing in the morning."

Her blood ran ice cold. "What?"

"We can walk up along the coastline toward The Freedom States. We can hunt for food. Find our own shelter along the way. Find some way to cross the border and...."

"Haven't you been listening to me? They'll come for us."

"It's too dangerous."

"I was here for two weeks before they found me...."

"I'm the one who left the cell phone and the note on the back porch, Hannah. I'm the one who phoned and instructed you to come to the beach that day. There is no Underground Railway here."

His confession hit her like a ton of bricks. Her head whirled with confusion. Her guts clenched into a sickening knot.

Jacob frowned. "Only a few days ago I had full intentions of killing you here. Of burying your body out back with the others who've escaped my father's Breeder Plantation."

"The others? You killed them?"

He shook his head.

"I haven't killed any of my father's Breeder Slaves, but I have killed others. Many of them. It's what I was trained to do."

The news that he'd killed people didn't come as a shock. She knew free men and women were trained to kill without questioning why. What interested her was that he'd watched her for two weeks with plenty of time to harm her. Yet he hadn't hurt her.

"The rumors about this deserted mansion were originally circulated by my father," he continued. "It makes the job easier for the Hitman when the slave runs. All the Breeder Plantation owners do it. Circulate rumors amongst the Slaves. It gives them somewhere to run if they decide to escape. It makes it easier for the Hitman to catch a runner when he knows where she's going. I knew you'd be coming here, Hannah. I saw you the instant you showed up. I dropped by every night and every morning to watch you the entire two weeks you were here. But I couldn't stay long because I was always being tracked."

"There is no Underground Railroad?" She still couldn't believe it. Couldn't believe that the Railroad was a lie.

"Not at this mansion."

"Why are you being so cruel? Why are you telling me all these horrible lies?"

"You were right when you told me I was a cold bastard the first day we met on the beach, Hannah. The Hit School trained me so well I had my finger on that trigger for two weeks. I had you in my sights." His voice was full of torture. Full of pain.

His pain sifted through her confusion, ripping away all her anger in one violent sweep.

Jacob Romero was baring his soul to her. Taking a chance that she would leave him. She had to prove to him she would never leave him. That telling her the truth wouldn't break her trust in him. She needed to show him she would never push him away.

"You didn't kill me, Jacob. You beat them. The Hit School. Your father. You're stronger than they are. You're free from them."

That awful dead look in his eyes began to fade, replaced by hope.

"You're not upset to find out there isn't an Underground Railroad?"

"Of course I'm upset."

The hope vanished from his eyes.

"But I'm glad you told me the truth, Jacob. It's just now I have a hollow feeling in my stomach. No one is coming to help us. We're all alone."

"We have each other. That's something, isn't it?" He smiled a somewhat wobbly smile.

"But we still aren't free."

Hannah rested her head on his warm chest and listened to his heart pounding against her ear.

His hand sifted through her hair, and he cupped the back of her neck, tilting her head upward.

"Our love will set us free."

His lips touched hers in a feather light kiss. Gathering her into his arms, he cradled her fiercely against his body. She knew he was still upset. She could feel it in the tight way he held her. So tight she feared he would crush her ribs.

But there wasn't anything she could say that would soothe him.

Stark reality had reared its ugly head. They were in danger here. Sooner or later someone would find them. Whether it was a Breeder Slave on the run or a Hitman or a Hitgal looking for them.

Sadness clutched at her heart as reality settled in around her. Jacob was right. Tomorrow morning they'd have to leave.

* * * *

Early the next morning, Jacob found Hannah sitting on the back porch. Her lovely body wrapped in a sheet, her bare legs dangling freely off the edge of the veranda as she watched a butterfly flutter nearby along the morning breeze.

Her hair was windswept, her cheeks rosy from the cool morning air. She looked so pretty he wanted to push her down onto the veranda, rip the sheet from her body, and fuck her senseless.

The severe frown marring her pretty face stopped him. It was a frown that speared pain straight into Jacob's heart and made him wish they could stay here at the mansion for a few more days.

He knew she didn't want to leave here. He didn't want to go either. So far no one had shown up, but, deep in his heart, he suspected his family had kept the place a secret from the Hitman Association. They would protect him, but they wouldn't protect Hannah. It would only be a matter of time before a deal was brokered. A deal that would keep Jacob safe but would kill Hannah.

He shuddered at that horrific thought. Without her he was a walking dead man. He wouldn't go on living. He would kill himself. It was as simple as that.

There was something else to consider. They had no transportation. Last night while Hannah had slept he'd stashed the car she'd stolen from his father in a nearby gulley and covered it with brush. They couldn't take the chance in using it.

Another fact had to be considered. Hannah had dumped his car miles up the beach. It was only a matter of time before it was found, and his fellow Hitmen and Hitgals would be swarming all over the site looking for clues. The Association had many sophisticated, top-secret ways of tracing tire tracks from the Hit car, even if the car had been driven on pavement. It was only a matter of time before they followed the tire tracks here.

"Morning," he called out.

She turned and smiled when she saw him standing in the doorway. To his disappointment the smile didn't reach those pretty green eyes.

"Morning," she whispered.

"I missed you when I woke up. Thought we could pick up where we left off before we fell asleep."

"I didn't want to wake you. Have you eaten?"

"Not hungry. How about you?"

She shook her head, turned away, and returned her attention to the orange-winged butterfly now fluttering around one of the nearby plants.

Jacob slid a hand over Hannah's warm shoulder and squeezed her tense muscles.

"You okay?"

She nodded, but from the angle of her face he noticed she wasn't okay. Especially when he saw the sparkling tears in her eyes.

Oh shit! The last thing he wanted was Hannah to start to cry. It would break his heart.

He sat down on the veranda beside her and ran his hand beneath the sheet. He stroked the warm silky flesh at the small of her naked back in a comforting motion.

"We don't have to go right now," he said. "We can wait a little while longer if you want?"

Her lower lip trembled. "No, you're right. We do have to go. We have to leave our home."

Those two words impacted him with such a warm feeling he could barely breath.

"We'll find another home. Somewhere safer than here."

"I know." A sexy smile tilted her luscious red lips, and Jacob's breath slammed up against his lungs. "But just in case something happens to us ... I want to feel your arms around me one last time. I want you deep inside me. I want you to make me feel safe for just a little while longer."

Without warning, she slipped the sheet off her shoulders and let it fall into a puddle on the veranda. Leaning back on her elbows, she allowed him full view of her curvy breasts.

Jacob's shaft hardened at the sight and wasted no time. Reaching out, he cupped her heavy breasts in each hand and with thumb and forefinger he twisted each juicy looking nipple.

He watched Hannah's eyes shut. Listened to her whimper with arousal. They were low sexy sounds that made Jacob's penis thicken even more.

He twisted her nipples until she cried out and her eyes flew open.

"Keep your eyes open, Hannah. I want you to watch me make love to your nipples."

She blinked. Her eyes full of arousal and understanding as Jacob's head lowered. He took one of her tight buds into his mouth.

The bead was hot and juicy as he nibbled with his teeth and tongued her areola before clamping his mouth over her breast like a suction cup. Her back arched against him and her whimpers made his erection ache with an intense need to fuck her.

Her breaths became labored and harsh as he continued to suckle. He moved from one breast to the other. An occasional cry ripped through the air as he continued to tenderly sink his teeth into her hard buds.

Once in awhile he'd stop and look up to make sure she was watching. Her pain-pleasure filled eyes were dazed but she saw how he worshipped her body.

Then he dived at her breasts again. Twisting those plump nipples between his thumb and forefinger, taking the quivering beads into his mouth and nipping them once in a while just to hear her erotic cries.

By the time he was finished her nipples were red and quivering, her breasts swollen and heaving with her every breath.

His hand settled onto her silky belly and dipped into that gorgeous belly button he loved to fiddle with. Probing there in an effort to feel how her abdominal and stomach muscles tensed up beneath his touch. It was a technique he'd discovered on his own. An area of arousal on a woman that was almost always neglected by men. But not by him.

He loved the feel of the warm indentation. Loved the idea that this was where Hannah had been secured in a woman's womb.

It reminded him that he would secure children in Hannah's

womb.

He would enjoy making her pregnant. Many times.

He could already imagine how sexy she'd look. Her belly big and round with his child. How hard her silky skin would feel beneath his hands as he cupped her swollen flesh.

During her pregnancy, he would make love to her and listen to those sweet sexy moans as he thrust deep inside her and suckled from her milk-laden breasts. And then after the child was born, and she was once again slender, he would keep fucking her until she was pregnant again.

He wanted lots of kids. Lots of little boys and girls of his own that he could teach how to play games, how to hunt and fish. And all the while he'd keep fucking Hannah because she was so beautiful and he loved her so much.

* * * *

There was an oddly beautiful look in Jacob's eyes as he finally lifted his mouth from her swelled red nipples.

A look that made love fill her heart.

"What are you thinking?" she asked as his fingers slid away from her aroused belly button and drew a teasing line over her abdomen across her mound to the outside edges of her quivering nether lips.

"I'm thinking about how much I love to fuck you. And how much I love you."

Hannah blinked with shock. He'd never said those words to her before. Never whispered them into her ears as he'd made love to her.

"Every time I look at you my heart swells with something I can't explain. I want to fuck you all the time. I love to listen to your gentle voice. I love the way you look at me with so much love in your eyes as I fuck you. I want to find us a safe place to live where no one will dictate to us who we will be and what kind of work we'll do."

Her heart thumped wildly at his confessions.

"And most of all I want to have children with you. Lots of them."

The familiar fear of being forced to produce offspring at an alarming rate ripped through Hannah.

"How many?" she asked, suddenly uncomfortable with the idea that she might already be pregnant by his seed.

"As many as you want."

"How many do you want?"

"It's up to you," he said.

The hot fingers at her clit slipped across her pleasure bud making her gasp as shards of arousal rippled through her cunt.

"Um. I haven't really thought about it. I mean, I've never thought of how many kids."

"How about six?" he asked.

Her eyes widened in shock, and he laughed.

"I'm the one who's going to have to carry the babies, y'know," she said seriously.

"You'll make a beautiful mother. And don't think for one minute you being pregnant will stop me from fucking you, Hannah."

She gasped at the intensity of desire flashing in his eyes.

"I love fucking a pregnant woman. No matter how far along she is."

A tinge of jealousy swirled through her. It was quickly extinguished as one long finger slid inside her cunt making her squirm with pleasure.

"And I suppose you've had your share of pregnant women?" she hissed as she tried to prevent another cry of pleasure from spilling out of her mouth.

"I've fucked a lot of pregnant Breeder Slaves, Hannah. But I've never fucked a pregnant woman that I love more than my own life."

His words overwhelmed her to the point where she didn't know what to say. Confusion gripped her. Yes, she was jealous he'd slept with other women. But he'd just said he loved her more than his own life. How could she deny him children if he felt so strongly about her?

She'd thought about having children. Especially when she'd been surrounded by pregnant Breeder Slaves for most of her life. But she'd also seen the dead looks in the mother's eyes after their newborns had been taken away.

She'd tried to get used to the idea of producing babies with the male Breeder Slaves or the other men who came to the Plantation. She'd also dreamed about how many she'd have when she was free. She'd always thought along the lines of two babies, maybe three.

But six?

Another strong masculine finger slipped inside her moist cunt making Hannah instinctively lift her hips to increase her pleasure.

His fingers penetrated deeper. He felt so good inside her. Made her feel so excited at the thought of what he was about to do to her.

But six children? The question dove into her mind again. Strangely enough the longer she thought about having six children with Jacob, the more she liked the idea.

"I think I could settle with four, maybe five."

"You're a demanding woman," he said as he slid another hot finger into her cunt. "I've only got four fingers on one hand."

Hannah laughed between gasps of arousal.

"I mean five children, not five fingers."

"Oh! Sure I knew that." He grinned sheepishly, slipped a forth finger inside her, and began to thrust slowly, keeping his eyes glued to her face as if watching for her reaction.

At the same time, he continued to massage her now ultra sensitive nub.

His head dipped, and she looked down to see her cherry colored nipple slip between his sensuous lips. His warm mouth invoked more waves of sensations through her body. Sharp teeth nipped at her aching breasts and nipples making her gasp with a combination of pain and pleasure. The pain was quickly extinguished as his tongue swirled over the tender areas he'd bitten.

"And when you're pregnant, I'll suckle the milk from your breasts, Hannah," he said as he took her other nipple into his hot mouth and nibbled roughly.

Hannah cried out at the fierceness of his mouth devouring her flesh. His fingers plunged frantically inside her cunt, and she could feel the juices flowing freely.

The shuddering of a massive orgasm began as her cunt muscles tightened around his fingers.

Without warning, he popped her aching nipple out of his mouth and withdrew his fingers from her spasming cunt.

Oh heavens! What was he doing?

She watched in bewilderment as he quickly scrambled down the veranda stairs and came around to stand between her legs. Within a slit second, he dropped his jagged green shorts, and she inhaled sharply as his massive love muscle stood erect and quite ready for duty.

The sight of his giant cockhead was intoxicating, and the arousing sight of the veins pulsing along his massive shaft made Hannah whimper as lust raced through her veins.

"I'm going to fuck you so much, it'll last you until we get to freedom," he stated.

Without warning, he grabbed her by the ankles and slid her a little closer to him until her ass hit the edge of the wooden porch and her legs nestled against his powerful hips. The sight of her long legs spread apart on each side of his hips made a heated anticipation rip through her body.

He reached out and ran a hot finger up along the opening of her clit. Hannah's pussy quivered at his touch.

"I can see you won't be needing any more priming. You're so damn wet for me."

"I'm always wet for you, Jacob."

He grinned at her words. It was a sexy grin that made her heart skip a beat.

"Let's try a different approach this time. Shall we?"

Puzzled yet excited, Hannah watched as he lifted her legs onto his muscular shoulders, hoisting her ass a few inches into the air, giving him easier access to her.

"This looks to be a delicious position," he whispered thickly.

Her heart hammered wildly in her chest as his giant cockhead slid erotically against her asshole and then rose to delicately part her nether lips.

His blue eyes blazed with passion, and his strong hands clasped her hips.

Hannah braced herself.

A split second later, he plunged his thick shaft deep into her wet and waiting cunt.

As he impaled her, the breath tore from her lungs. Hannah grabbed onto his bare wrists for support, digging her fingernails deeply into his skin, ignoring his wince of pain. Instinctively, she clamped her legs around Jacob's neck and squeezed tightly. The movement made more room for him, and he drove his rod deeper than it had ever been before.

It filled her to bursting. Stretched her impossibly as his thick rod slammed into sensitive areas he'd never hit before.

He withdrew in an agonizingly slow movement that left her gasping in earnest as she awaited his re-entry. She didn't have long to wait.

His bulging erection thrust deep inside her. The entire eight inches plunged valiantly along her hot channel, reawakening all her arousal centers, creating violent stirrings of an oncoming orgasm.

He must have felt she was on the edge of a climax because his pumping eased off ever so slightly, keeping her gasping for breath and anxiously waiting for him to bring her to a quick fulfillment.

But she knew she wouldn't get her wish.

He wanted this to last a long time for her. And for himself.

Her grip around his wrists tightened as he continued to pump more slowly.

Deep, long, hard strokes that made her whimper with both pain and pleasure.

The strength and torturous slowness of his thrusts were amazing. Her cunt muscles clenched around his hot flesh every time he began to withdraw as if she were trying to keep him from leaving her.

Guttural moans of desire escaped his lips. The sound of it like music to her ears.

The pleasure his thick intrusion created made her forget the sadness claiming her about leaving here. Once they were finished making love they would have to leave. It was as if he was thinking the same thing. As if he wanted to make love to her forever.

Once again he picked up his pace. Shooting his hard penis into her like a massive battering ram. His tight balls slapped frantically against her ass turning her on even higher.

She heard him groan again as he pulled out of her and then slammed back inside.

Every time he entered her cunt his penis seemed to be hotter, thicker, filling her even more than the last plunge.

Desperation began to edge his thrusts. His penis thickened, and it shuddered inside her. She knew he was going to climax soon.

Opening her eyes, she watched the arousal flood his features. Perspiration drenched his forehead. Tiny muscles in his tightly clenched jaws spasmed wildly. And the cute way his eyes scrunched as he orgasmed inside her made her heart leap with joy.

But he didn't release his load.

One of the delicious rumors that had circulated was he'd trained himself to have multiple orgasms without ejaculating.

The rumors had been true. She'd experienced that aspect many times during their lovemaking sessions yesterday, and she was experiencing it once again.

His face grew serene as the climax passed. Yet he continued to pump into her, keeping her on the edge of bliss. Making her gasp and whimper at the onslaught of his hard masculine thrusts.

By now Hannah's cunt was totally soaked. She could feel the wetness of her cum leaking out of her. Could smell the sweet scent of her arousal drifting all around her. Her cunt muscles clenched at his hot penis, holding him tightly inside her as pleasure waves exploded yet again through her body.

This time her body shuddered with an orgasm like no other she'd ever experienced. Stars and blackness hovered at the sides of her vision as wave after violent wave of pleasure swallowed her whole, making her cry out at each impact.

She felt her limbs go weak at the assaulting pleasure. Felt her cunt spasm frantically around his thick rod as she sailed away into pleasure land.

From somewhere far away and a long time later, she heard Jacob's tense shouts as he finally came inside her, spurting his hot love seed deep into her very core.

Chapter Eight

"Hannah!" A rough shaking on her naked shoulder zipped through her sex-induced nap with such a fervor she snapped her eyes open and gasped at the fear sparking Jacob's eyes.

He pressed a warm finger to her lips and whispered, "Someone's inside the house."

Horrible shivers of terror ripped away any remnants of sleep.

Grabbing her hand and the sheet, he yanked her off the porch. Her tender feet slapped against painful sharp rocks, but she clamped down on a cry. In one violent jerk, he pulled her behind a sidewall of the stone mansion.

It wasn't a moment too soon because the back door creaked open and light footsteps clomped across the wooden veranda where Jacob had just made love to her.

Her heart hammered violently against her chest as Jacob draped the sheet around her shoulders. From out of nowhere, his gun appeared in his hand.

"Who do you think it is?" she whispered through chattering teeth.

Jacob shook his head and said nothing.

Fear etched his eyes. His jaw was clenched tight. A muscle twitched wildly in his cheek. He looked as if he were a man ready to kill. The thought made her shiver. The approaching footsteps made her tremble even harder.

Jacob's hand pressed firmly against her belly, pushing her behind him, protecting her from whoever was now descending the steps.

Hannah held her breath and peered over his shoulder. Her heart stopped the instant she saw a gun attached to a very large hand poke around the corner.

Jacob didn't waste any time.

He grabbed the deadly pistol and yanked the intruder into the open.

Within a blink of an eye, it was all over.

A dark-haired man clad in the standard army green Hitman uniform lay sprawled on his back in the dust. His eyes blinked wildly up at them as Jacob pressed both the intruder's gun and his own gun firmly against the man's forehead.

To Hannah's surprise, the intruder chuckled. No hint of fear showed in his fudge brown eyes. Nor did he appear concerned at the guns pointed firmly against his head. He acted as if he trusted Jacob not to pull the trigger.

Jacob, on the other hand, seemed to be taking the matter very seriously. Tenseness quivered the muscles in his bare shoulders. Waves of angry heat washed out of him, slamming into Hannah, sending signals of alarm shooting throughout her body.

"Give me one fucking reason why I shouldn't pull the trigger, you back stabbing son of a bitch," Jacob growled.

"Cause I'm your best friend?"

"You were my best friend, Tool. And now you're a talking corpse."

"I take it this must be Hannah?" The man looked up at her with an amusing twinkle in his eyes. "I'd shake hands, but I'll save the introductions for later."

His gaze swung back to Jacob. The smile drifted off Tool's lips, and he said rather seriously, "We need to talk. Privately."

To Hannah's surprise, Jacob nodded and pulled the guns away from Tool's forehead.

"I'll meet you out front."

Tool nodded. In an instant, he was on his feet, wiping the dust off his backside as he grinned at Hannah.

"Pleased to meet you, Hannah."

With a burst of energy, he ascended the porch stairs and casually crossed the veranda toward the open door.

Hannah's heart pounded violently against her chest as she watched Tool disappear into the darkness of the mansion.

"Why in the world did you let him go?"

"If he wanted us dead, we'd be dead by now," he said coldly.

He grabbed her hand and slapped the warm handle of his gun into her palm and curled her fingers around it.

"If something happens to me, don't hesitate to use this."

"I can't shoot anyone." She tried to shove the deadly weapon back to him.

"You can, and you will. The safety catch is off. I need you to back me up. He tries anything, point the gun at his head, and pull the trigger. It's as simple as that."

The firmness in his voice had Hannah nodding obediently.

He grabbed her other hand and pulled her up the stairs and into the cool interior of the mansion.

* * * *

Jacob's legs trembled as he stepped out the front door into the shadowy overhang with Tool's gun clutched firmly in his hand.

Immediately, he spotted Tool leisurely leaning against the hood of his car, his arms crossed casually over his chest. He looked as if he didn't have a care in the world.

But looks could be deceiving.

Sure, it was strange Tool had arrived in daylight. It was also suspicious that he had allowed his gun to be taken away so easily.

Tool was one of the best Hitmen in the field. He'd been on office duty monitoring the tracking devices simply because he was recovering from a bullet wound he'd suffered when he'd been training a Hitgal how to shoot. A Hitgal Tool had fallen head over heels in love with, clouding his judgment, and hence him getting shot and getting office duty.

Unfortunately, Jacob had taken advantage of Tool being in charge of the trackers, and Tool had turned him in.

The raw anger of betrayal zinged along Jacob's nerves again, making his heart pound insanely.

He squinted his eyes and surveyed the surrounding buttercup riddled meadows and hillside for evidence that Tool had brought along some sort of welcoming party.

"I'm alone!" Tool called out when he spotted Jacob lurking in the shadowy alcove.

"You better be. Because if you aren't, you'll be the first one I take down with me."

"You already know I wouldn't have let you take my gun if I didn't want you to."

Jacob's insides shook with indecision. Should he simply kill Tool right now, grab Hannah, and get the hell out of here?

Or should he hear what Tool had to say?

He took dead aim at Tool's head and stepped out into the warm sunshine. Keeping the gun lined on his target, Jacob walked the twenty feet until he stood directly in front of him.

"You know why I'm here, don't you?" Tool asked.

He didn't so much as acknowledge the gun pointed at his face.

"I have my suspicions." Jacob's fingers itched on the trigger. If he had to, he'd kill Tool in order to save Hannah and feel no pangs of guilt about doing it.

"Your family is talking about making a deal with the Hitman Association."

Jacob's guts twisted in agony. "What kind of deal?"

"They want to turn Hannah over to the Association if the Association spares your life. Your family told me this might be one of the places you could be hiding. Before they finalize the deal, they want me to locate you first, then go back and tell them without letting you know of course."

"You going to tell them?"

"They promised me a million green ones if I did as they asked."

"That all?"

Tool grinned. "You think mighty highly of yourself and that woman in there. I must admit she's quite a good-looking woman. She the one who's been on your mind all these years?"

"She's the one."

Tool's grin widened.

Jacob allowed himself to relax a bit.

"Why did you turn me in, Tool?"

Raw pain sheared through Tool's eyes, and instantly Jacob realized he'd been wrong about him. Guilt ripped through his guts like a lancing sword.

"I'm sorry I doubted you, Tool. It's just when Sawblade showed up...."

"No apologies, Jake. I would have thought the same thing under the circumstances."

"What happened?"

"Good question. Near as I can figure, when I diverted the tracker system from your car to shadow another Hitman working in the area, I triggered some internal alarm that no one bothered to tell me about. The alarm got picked up. Within minutes of the divert, all hell broke loose, and I had them up my ass. No time to warn you. They stashed me into isolation. Interrogated me. I told them you wanted some down time because you'd hooked up with a woman. Anyways, they diverted the tracker back onto your car and sent Sawblade over to the hotel to help you with the hit that got away."

"He found us."

"I heard."

Tool's gaze slid to the two inches of white bandage peeking out from beneath Jacob's tattered green shorts.

"War wounds on your leg." His eyes traveled to Jacob's wrists. To the scratches Hannah had branded him with when she'd dug her nails into his flesh while he'd pounded his aching shaft into her.

"More injuries on your wrists, shoulders, and back. Looks like you've had a tough time of it."

Jacob's face suddenly flushed with embarrassment at Tool's knowing grin.

"The entire Hit Association is turning over every stone trying to find you. Doesn't look good for them that a Hitman and a Breeder Slave hooked up together. I guess you realize you've got a hit on your head."

Jacob nodded.

"I'm glad I finally found you. I got a plan. You want to hear it?"

The last two sentences were spoken so casually it took Jacob a few seconds before it fully sank in that Tool was offering to help them.

Jacob nodded and lowered his weapon.

* * * *

Hannah clutched the gun tighter as she watched Tool get into his car.

Although she didn't know how to use the weapon, she felt reasonably sure she would have shot Tool had he made the slightest suspicious move. There was no way in the world she would ever let anyone hurt her man.

Poking the gun out a crack in the glass of a dirty window, she'd aimed directly at Tool, her finger lodged on the trigger just like Jacob had suggested.

The two men had talked for a good twenty minutes. For the first few minutes, they'd been very serious. Then Jacob had lowered the weapon, and Hannah had been tenser than a cat on a hot tin roof as she'd wondered what they were discussing.

The front door creaked open and broke Hannah from her thoughts.

She hurried over to meet him.

"What did he want?" she asked when he stepped into the barren living room.

"You know what? You look so damn good I could start eating you on the spot."

He took her into his arms and tried to kiss her, but she quickly shoved him away.

"What the hell is wrong with you? You just let him leave. What did he want? What is he doing here?"

"He's here to help us."

"Bullshit! He's a Hitman, same as you. He's here to take us in. I'm packing. We're leaving."

"We're staying." His voice sounded so calm, Hannah thought

he'd snapped.

"You're insane."

"I like being insane. It's more fun this way." He reached out for her, and this time she allowed him to take her into his arms. Once again he tried to kiss her. She turned her head away in defiance.

"What did he want?"

"To help us."

"And you believed him?"

"We can trust him. If we couldn't, we'd be dead by now."

"But you said he's the one who turned you in."

"It was a misunderstanding. Right now we've got to pack."

"You just said we're staying."

"We are. But we're going to have to abandon the house. It'll only be for a few hours until Tool comes back for us."

"What's going on? Where are we going?"

"Go upstairs and take only what you need. Hide the rest. Hide it good so no one knows we were here. I'll take care of everything down here. I'll explain later."

The excitement in Jacob's voice was contagious, and Hannah headed for the stairs.

"Hannah?"

She turned around.

The teasing smile on his face made her breath back up in her lungs.

"Don't forget the dildo. We're going to need it."

* * * *

Uneasiness intermingled with pleasure as Hannah tried hard not to squirm beneath Jacob's arousing touches. He'd brought her down to the same secluded little love nest by the beach that they'd used all day yesterday.

Tall grass swayed lazily all around them, hiding them from view.

He'd also tried to reassure her that for now they were safe.

Hannah, on the other hand, was feeling a tad bit uneasy as she listened to the ocean waves lap gently against the sandy beach, half expecting to hear footsteps of many Hitmen sift through the nearby sand.

Thank goodness the only witness watching what Jacob was doing to her was the warm sun slowly climbing into the blue sky.

He'd already aroused her breasts by suckling them, pinching, and biting. And now Jacob had started his seductive ministrations elsewhere on her body in an effort to keep her calm.

Well, maybe calm was the wrong word.

Occupied might be a better word.

His thumb slid erotically over her clit, making her cunt moisten with a powerful need for him. The mini orgasms he created as he gently finger fucked her was having a damaging impact on the serious conversation she was trying to carry on with him.

"Are you sure you can trust him? Are you sure he won't come back with an entire Hit Squad?" She bit out as a second masculine finger slipped erotically into her wet cunt.

"He's going to secure a reliable car for us and some ID so we can cross the border to The Free States."

Shock pushed aside her uneasiness. "The Free States? You're kidding? Why didn't you tell me earlier?"

"I had other things on my mind. Like getting you in the mood."

Another long hot finger slipped inside her, and a small orgasm ripped through her body.

He grinned. The smoky desire clouding his eyes as he continued to massage her pleasure bud made her body sizzle with heat and want.

"Tool's going to get us through to safety. You'll see. We can trust him. He's got someone at the border working for him."

It was getting increasingly difficult to concentrate on questioning him with all these mini orgasms ripping through her body, but she wouldn't stop this pleasure for the world. She just wished he would put her curiosity to ease so she could really get into his lovemaking.

"I don't understand. How can a Hitman have someone working at the border for him?"

"He's got resources, Hannah. I can't tell you anymore than that. Not yet. Just know that we can trust him. By now, he's spread the word that we've crossed the border. They won't be looking too hard for us anymore. Meanwhile, do you like cold weather?"

"Not really. How do you know that he spread the word that we aren't in The States anymore?"

"Its part of the plan he outlined to me."

"What plan?"

"Hannah, don't worry about it. Let's just enjoy ourselves. Please?"

"You sound like you're begging."

"That's because I am. Begging to fuck you. Now, you didn't answer my question."

"What question?"

"Do you like cold weather?"

"No, why?"

"From what I hear, it's cold north of the border, and we're going to have to keep each other warm."

"I like the sound of that."

"Thought you would. You know what?"

"What?"

His thumb stopped massaging, and his hand slowly withdrew his cream drenched fingers from her cunt.

"I'm really thirsty."

The fire in his bright blue eyes and the sight of his stone hard rod encouraged moistness to drip from between her legs. The blood in her veins began to boil with anticipation.

Turning slightly, she lifted her knees up and spread her legs wider, allowing Jacob easier access to her.

"Drink away," she whispered and wiggled her hips invitingly.

He didn't hesitate. Dipping his head between her legs, his hot breath caressed her moist clit, and she almost climaxed on the spot.

"Are you sure we can trust him?" she gasped.

He chuckled. "You've already asked that question. Try not to worry. He's going to come through for us, Hannah. I've known him for four years. From what I've seen, he's good at his job."

"So are you," she said softly.

Goodness the man had a tongue of a God. Long and lethal. And oh so powerful. His tongue thrusts were strong and hard, and the intense way he sucked at her clit made the rumblings of another orgasm begin deep within her woman's core.

Suddenly he withdrew.

"Don't stop!" she cried out in desperation.

His head lifted, and he grinned wickedly at her.

"I've got a surprise for you, Hannah. Something very special. But first, I want you to get on your hands and knees, legs spread wide, face down, ass up in the air so I can get a good look at you."

His dark voice wrapped around her in enticing waves. It excited her. Aroused her. At this point, she would do anything to get relief from the intense desire he'd unleashed inside her body with his tongue.

Quickly, she got into the position he wanted. Her head down toward the blanket, her ass high in the air, legs spread like he'd instructed.

"I didn't want to do this to you just yet. Not until I had a chance to give you some time to get used to this idea ... but because I don't know how much time we have..." A tiny shiver of fear scrambled up her spine at his words. "I want to show you so much pleasure, Hannah. Pleasure you never knew existed."

The fear flushed away, replaced with the heated arousal again.

Was he kidding? Every time he made love to her he brought her such exquisite pleasure she'd never known something like it existed.

From behind her she could hear him stand up. A moment later, his large hands smoothed some of the warm yarrow healing oil over her ass cheeks.

"You're ass is so velvety, so beautiful." His words were soft and tender, his warm hands expertly caressing her curves.

The first stirrings of arousal rippled through her as a well-lubricated finger nudged against her anal hole.

"I want to take you, Hannah. I want to take you with the dildo in your cunt and me inside your sweet ass. I want to fill you up like you've never been filled before."

Hannah's heart thundered against her chest at the thought of being double penetrated.

She'd heard the Breeder Slaves whisper about how several Romero brothers would bring exquisite joy to one Breeder Slave.

Once Hannah had come upon a trio of Romero brothers fucking her best friend, Lara, another Breeder Slave. Agonized pleasure had scrunched up her friend's face. The brothers had arranged Lara in such a way that as they stood she was sandwiched between two muscular Romero brothers. One pounded his huge rod into her rear while another brother had fucked her from the front. Sounds of frantic slurping had come from Lara's mouth as she'd worked away on a third brother's massive rod with her passion swelled lips.

The mesmerizing sight had unleashed a dark, searing arousal inside Hannah's body.

From the shadows, she'd watched totally enthralled as the men made love to Lara. Their masculine grunts intermingled with her sweet feminine cries of arousal.

Hannah had found herself wishing they would see her. Wished they would invite her to join them, but they hadn't seen her. Even if they had, they wouldn't have invited her to join in the festivities. It was known throughout the Plantation that Hannah belonged exclusively to Simon until such a time as he decided to part with her.

Later that same night, Lara confided in Hannah that she'd seen her watching them. Lara had also confessed she loved to be fucked by three men. She was addicted to the Romero brothers and the pleasure they inflicted upon her.

Dangerous arousal had coursed through Hannah at Lara's words. But Hannah had kept her secret fantasy to be taken by two or three men to herself. It was just a dark fantasy and nothing more.

Interestingly enough, Jacob was going to make her fantasy come true.

Hannah smiled inwardly. She was glad she'd fallen in love with a man who enjoyed variety in his sex life.

"You're so tight, Hannah. So achingly tight. I can't wait to fuck you. To pleasure you." Around and around his fingers went, creating circles of sensual pleasure wherever he touched. Every once in a while a finger or two or even three dipped inside her anal hole, just a little deeper every time creating whispers of pleasure with every seductive stroke.

Strange sensations blossomed inside her ass, spreading toward her cunt like a wildfire.

Suddenly, she felt the thick head of her dildo press against the opening to her drenched cunt. Before she could mentally prepare herself, Jacob impaled her with the dildo in one deep thrust.

The unexpected fullness left her gasping for air and moaning for more.

Slowly, he pulled it back out again. She could hear the suctioning sound as her cunt muscles tried to keep the thick intrusion inside her. Could feel the excited quivers of her cunt as he slammed the dildo back inside.

Soon he was plunging in and out of her, and at the same time his hot flesh probed at her back door.

The excitement at the thought of one of her darkest fantasies coming to life was overwhelming. Thrusting her hips backward, she urged him to hurry it up.

His teasing chuckle penetrated through her layers of arousal. It frustrated her and made her a little angry.

"Jacob! Please hurry," she found herself gasping.

She groaned in frustration as the dildo poised inside the mouth of her cunt.

An erotic grunt ripped loose from Jacob. Hannah's breath hitched at the primal sound, and she gasped as his lubricated member slid slowly into the tight passage of her anus.

Immediately, she realized this was going to be a different experience. An experience unlike any she'd ever had before.

The heat of Jacob's member curled through her ass like a hard poker of fire, creating sparkles of dark agony and sweet pleasures that left her craving for more.

His thick cock filled her ass, stretching her muscles with such a sinful desire she threw her head back and cried out at its threatening intensity.

"That's right, Hannah. Enjoy it! Enjoy the sensations." Jacob slammed the massive dildo deep into her cunt again, making a wonderful soul wrenching ecstasy wrench her body. At the same time, he pounded his thick rod harshly into her backside, filling her like she'd never been filled before. Stuffing her with such agonizing and incredible sensations she couldn't help but slip into a dark world. A dream world that eased away all her fears and filled her body with wonderful explosions and tidal waves of sizzling pleasures. A dark world that had her body convulsing wildly and her mind shattering into wonderful splinters of love, desire, and sensual cravings.

* * * *

"Bang! You're dead." The masculine voice curled through Hannah's layers of sleep, prodding her awake.

At first, she didn't realize the meaning of what had just been said. But when she opened her eyes and saw Jacob's friend Tool looking down at them, a gun held precariously in his hand, panic zipped through her veins, making Hannah bolt up.

The blanket covering her body slipped downward, revealing her breasts to the stranger.

Tool's eyes widened in amusement and an appreciation that made Hannah blush despite her fear.

Grabbing the sheet, she covered herself and shook Jacob's shoulder.

In an instant, Jacob's eyes flickered open.

When he saw the gun in Tool's hand, he cursed violently.

Tool shook his head slowly. "You are really losing your touch, Jake. It's time for you to retire."

To Hannah's surprise, he dangled the barrel of the gun from his fingers as if it were a dead mouse then threw the weapon onto the blankets covering Jacob's lap.

It was quickly followed by a package.

"This the stuff?" Jacob asked as he eagerly tore open the package, acting as if Tool hadn't just scared the turnips out of both of them.

"It's all there. You two better get ready to go because there isn't much time. My contact is in place at the border, but only for another two hours. It takes an hour and a half to get there. Grab what you need, I'll wait in the car."

Tool threw Hannah a grin and said, "You take good care of Jacob."

"I will."

"Don't be long."

Hannah nodded.

The instant Tool left, Hannah scrambled out from beneath the blanket. Hurriedly, she picked up Jacob's clothes and threw them at him.

"C'mon, get dressed. You heard the man."

"How about one more quick fuck before we leave?" He reached out and pulled her down onto his naked length.

His thick penis pulsed between her legs, and she couldn't help but be aroused.

"Tool said we had to hurry," she breathed as anxiety intermingled with desire.

"So we'll hurry."

His mouth came down on hers with a desperate need. Hannah moaned as his fingers slipped between her legs to fondle her clit.

She gasped into his mouth when his thumb lightly caressed her pleasure nub. She was wet within seconds.

All thoughts of freedom melted away the moment he entered her.

* * * *

"Shit!" Tool pounded the steering wheel of his car as they drew closer to the border patrol gate.

Hannah stiffened in alarm.

"What's wrong?" Jacob asked.

"She's not there."

"Turn the car around." The alarm in Jacob's voice sent icy shards of fear ripping through Hannah.

"If I do that, then we'll never have another chance as good as tonight. Besides, I turn around now, it'll draw attention to us. The ID's are good forgeries, but we don't need the extra attention."

Hannah curled tighter against the back seat. Her thoughts tumbled in a waterfall of confusion and fear. She wished like crazy that Jacob were back here with her. Wished he could soothe away the tremors of fear.

But he wasn't.

He was up front with Tool.

The grim outline of both their faces made perspiration form on her neck. A bead rolled down between her shoulder blades.

They drew closer to the Border Patrol.

Hannah inhaled a deep breath of the stuffy car air, trying to calm herself.

It didn't work.

She fought the sudden urge to bolt. She had no business involving Jacob and Tool in her flight for freedom. No right to ruin these two men's lives if they were caught with her in the car.

"Are you okay?" Jacob's soothing voice shattered her impending panic.

She nodded quickly and plastered a somewhat wobbly smile onto her face.

"Atta girl. It'll be over soon."

Jacob returned his attention to the front, leaving Hannah alone with the familiar panic rising inside her again.

How in the world had she ever allowed them to help her? They would get killed because of her selfishness and her desire for freedom.

The car rolled to a sudden stop.

Hannah just about jumped out of her skin when Tool lowered the window and a Border Guard dressed in an official looking blue uniform peeked his head inside.

"Your ID's please."

Tool, who looked as calm as a cucumber, handed him their new ID's.

The guard, a young man of about twenty, scrutinized the pictures on the Identification cards. ID cards that Tool had secured so quickly for them.

Jacob had told her Tool had risked his life going into Hitman Headquarters to get their pictures from the files.

If they ever got out of The States, she'd owe these two men big time.

Suddenly, the Border Patrol guard's dark eyes narrowed, and he looked at her.

Her pulse exploded.

Despite trying not to, Hannah tensed. She could feel the cold perspiration dot her forehead. Could feel the bitter taste of freedom slipping away.

The guard studied her until she wiggled nervously in the car seat.

To her surprise he said, "Welcome to the Free States, Hannah."

Tool swore softly, and Hannah's stomach did a dramatic flip.

"Why the hell didn't you tell me you were one of us? What happened to Cara? Why isn't she at her post?" Tool hissed.

"She was arrested a couple of hours ago. Someone must have found out about her, tipped off the authorities. They took her away."

"Son of a bitch! Do they have her in the back room?" Tool made a move to open the door, but the guard pushed his body against the door, preventing Tool from getting out.

"She's not here. Just stay calm. If you make a scene, the entire Railroad will be compromised."

Hannah blinked in surprise and confusion.

These men worked for the Underground Railroad?

Did Jacob know? He didn't seem surprised. Tool must have told him while outlining his plan back at the mansion earlier this morning.

"He's right, Tool," Jacob's voice was strangled. "Don't attract any attention."

The guard pretended to fiddle with the ID's, but now Hannah could see his eyes were darting around nervously.

He spoke quickly, "If they break her, she'll talk. You're her main contact. You aren't safe here anymore. You'll have to go with Hannah and the Hitman. I've slipped your new ID beneath theirs. Just forget about Cara. She's as good as dead."

Hannah pulsed quickened with fear for the woman she'd never heard of or seen before.

"I'm going back for her," Tool said between gritted teeth.

"You knew the rules when you signed up, Tool. So did Cara. Let's just keep this strictly professional for the sake of the Railroad."

Tool nodded numbly.

Hannah's throat seized up at the brightness of tears shining in Tool's dark eyes.

She felt the bitter sting of tears in her eyes, too. Tool was suffering terribly. And it was all her fault. All because she wanted her freedom.

"You're entering the Free States on permanent visas," the guard continued and handed Tool back the ID's, "Use them wisely."

"I'm going to deliver these two according to plan. But then I'm coming back in for her."

"If you do, Tool, you won't come back out alive. The

Underground can't afford to have you on the inside like a loose cannon. They'll take you down, just like they'll take care of Cara if the Border Guards don't do it first. Is that understood?"

Tool didn't say anything.

"Get the hell out of here, and don't come back." The Border Guard slapped the car door and waved them ahead.

Tool slammed the car into drive. Within seconds, he crossed the border and drove into the Free States.

Hannah should have been deliriously happy that she was free. She should have felt thrilled that she wouldn't have to endure the rest of her life being shared among men or producing babies at an alarming rate.

She should be happy that she could live the rest of her life with her very own sweet man.

Her gaze flew to Tool.

He gazed straight ahead as he drove in a quiet zombie-like state.

Obviously, his mind was on the woman named Cara. Hannah wondered what would happen to her during her interrogation. She wondered what kind of torture she would endure because of Hannah's need for freedom.

She wondered what kind of relationship Cara and Tool had. They must have had something special for Tool to want to risk his life and go back to The States to get her.

Hannah swung her gaze to Jacob and found him staring at her.

"You okay?"

Hannah nodded.

"We're free." His voice should have been happy, but he sounded tired and sad.

"We're free," Hannah agreed.

But how free was she?

Her insides rumbled with guilt at leaving behind so many Breeder Slaves.

Men and women like herself who wanted to attain their own freedom. People who wished to pursue their own dreams. People trapped in The States with no way out.

No escape except with the help of courageous men like Tool.

The End

Printed in the United States
49800LVS00001B/78